THE
MIDNIGHT
HUNT

BENJAMIN READ & LAURA TRINDER

2 PALMER STREET, FROME, SOMERSET BA11 1DS

Story: Trindles & Read
Words: Read

Text © Read Books Ltd 2021
Interior illustrations © Laura Trinder 2021
Cover illustration © Hannah Peck 2021

First published in Great Britain in 2021
Chicken House
2 Palmer Street
Frome, Somerset BA11 1DS
United Kingdom
www.chickenhousebooks.com

Chicken House/Scholastic Ireland, 89E Lagan Road, Dublin Industrial Estate,
Glasnevin, Dublin D11 HP5F, Republic of Ireland

Benjamin Read & Laura Trinder have asserted their right under the Copyright,
Designs and Patents Act 1988 to be identified as the authors of this work.

Cover and interior design by Steve Wells
Cover illustration by Hannah Peck
Interior illustrations by Laura Trinder
Typeset by Dorchester Typesetting Group Ltd
Printed and bound in Great Britain by CPI Group (UK) Ltd, Croydon CR0 4YY

FSC
www.fsc.org
MIX
Paper from
responsible sources
FSC® C020471

1 3 5 7 9 10 8 6 4 2

British Library Cataloguing in Publication data available.

PB ISBN 978-1-912626-88-5
eISBN 978-1-913696-22-1

*For my very own Emily, who might even
get around to reading it one day.*
– BR

For Chris, who makes the Daylight realm magical.
– LT

'Until at length the full moon, lustre-fraught,
Burst thro' the gloom wherein she was enshrined;
And then the willing, active, rapid thought
Around the past, as round the future twined,
At midnight hour.'

– JOHANN WOLFGANG VON GOETHE
'At Midnight Hour'

CHAPTER 1

It wasn't an obvious day for something terrible to happen, but maybe they never are. If they were obvious, people would just go, 'Oh, it's a Terrible Happenings type of day, better stay in bed', or something. That Saturday morning, when Emily came down fashionably late for breakfast, the only sign of terribleness was that her mum was making bacon sandwiches. This was highly suspicious though. It wasn't that her mum, Maeve, was a bad cook (although she absolutely was), but this was her dad's job. Had been for her whole life. Every Saturday, he'd be there dishing the bacon goodness out, after his shift at the Night Post. On this particular morning, however, he was slumped at the table, pale as one of the ghosts he delivered to.

'Dad, what is it? Are you okay?'

He looked up, and smiled a thin, watery smile.

'I'm okay, Puzzle, it's just that—'

'It's *just* that he's been *fired* by the blasted eejits at the Night Post,' her mum interrupted in her broad Irish accent, 'and kicked him out of the Midnight Hour they have, and taken his blasted key too!' She was yelling by the end, her face bright red.

The Midnight Hour was a whole other Victorian London, frozen in time when Big Ben first tolled midnight in 1859. It was now a sanctuary for all the remaining monsters and magic, but also a home from home for Emily and her whole deeply odd family.

'It's an outrage, that's what it is!' shouted Maeve. Emily's magical Pooka mum whacked the bacon spatula on to the worktop to punctuate her words. 'A piece of my mind I'd have given them, ye can be sure.'

She coughed suddenly as the smoke of burning bacon fat wafted from the grill. She was cursing at the cooker when a terrible noise erupted from under the table. It was the devil-baby (as Emily generally thought of her new brother), the latest, very unexpected arrival in the Featherhaugh household. Her dad, Alan, picked him up from his carrycot and rocked him. He normally quieted down because her dad had a very calming presence, but today he just kept screaming, while Alan looked hunched and sad.

Emily was rigid with shock. Her quiet and capable dad was an unflappable, immovable part of her universe. To see him so lost was . . . a lot.

'What do you mean, you've been fired?'

'I'm out of the Night Post. Strictly no "daysies", apparently.'

'Daysie' was a nasty word some of the Night Folk used for people from the Daylight world. He sagged back down into his chair, rubbing the back of the baby screaming in his arms.

'Everything's changing in there. They're cutting all connections with the outside.'

'Who's "they"?' demanded Emily.

'Those toffee-nosed, grey-faced, dried-up, dusty, Dead eejits that think they run the world!' shouted her mum from amidst a cloud of bacon smoke.

The Dead actually did kind of run the other world. However, after all her adventures in the Midnight Hour, Emily had friends in even higher places. She smacked her fist on the table.

'Right, well, I'll go straight in tonight and talk to the Library and get all this sorted out!'

'Love, I don't think you understand. You won't be going in. None of us will be.' Her dad sighed. 'They haven't just

fired me – they've sealed the doors between our worlds.'
His face was bleak and drawn.

'We're locked out of the Midnight Hour for good.'

And that was it. They were out, like they'd never been in.

Emily had railed and ranted and roared, but it was done. It wasn't like she hadn't given it her best shot, either. As the midnight chimes of Big Ben whispered down the Thames, they'd tried her mum's magic shadow key on the door of the local church. Nothing. They'd used her dad's supply of magic stamps to write letters of complaint to powerful friends. Nothing. Even one of the precious express delivery stamps, which would usually vanish at the stroke of midnight by magical collection, was still sat there in the morning.

That had been the final straw for her dad. He'd taken to the sofa and hadn't even glanced at his beloved compost heap since. He clumped around and had dinners with them and looked after the baby, but some essential spark seemed to have gone – he had, after all, done the world's most dangerous job, and without it, he didn't seem to know who he was supposed to be.

Emily knew how he felt. She yearned for the Hour. Usually, she was allowed to go in on school holidays and was due a half-term trip to visit Mammy Espeth, her mum's mum, clan chief of the Pooka and Emily's absolutely-must-never-be-called Nan. With Mammy's training, Emily had almost mastered her horse shape. Being half Pooka meant Emily was a shapeshifter and could do weird things with luck magic, but only inside the Midnight Hour, because there wasn't any magic left out here in the real world. In the Hour she was special, but out here she was just . . . Emily.

It was the worst of times, it was the . . . worst of times. It was like she'd been gifted something precious then had it snatched away from her. If she wasn't magic, what was she? It reminded her of the way that moody lion had kept kicking the kids out of Narnia. She'd always hated those bits. Them stuck outside, not knowing if they were ever going to be allowed back in, slowly starting to think they might have made it all up. She had imagined them stood at the back of a wardrobe, all hot and stuffy with horrid fur coats, but there being nothing there other than cobwebs and wooden boards. She used to worry every time she put the magic key in the Night Post door, that this would be the time it wouldn't turn and she'd be stuck outside for ever. Now her fears had come true.

Two weeks after the Bad News Breakfast, Emily was hiding upstairs in her bedroom. She'd had a near humdinger of a row with her mum and had retreated to prevent the apocalypse. They had a track record of catastrophic blowouts, as they both possessed an unstoppable family mouth condition known as the gob. Emily knew her mum had a lot on her plate, what with the baby and now a sad dad at home all day, but she was miserable too and it was hard not to snap sometimes. Now, hours later, she lay slumped on top of her bed, and watched the circular sculpture of the three black glass hares she called the Abbits chase their tails on her wall.

She sighed and fiddled with the necklace of old coins around her neck. They chinked and gleamed on their chain, all silver and gold and malice. Not just any old coins, but the Bad Pennies. They were the most ferociously cursed coins of all time, bearers of incredible ill-fortune, unless you were a luck-juggling Pooka like Emily, of course. Her mum (when in a better mood) had let her have them to cheer her up, but right now they were just another reminder of the magic she was missing. She lay back, clinking the coins, and tried to think happy Pooka thoughts. Darting through soft grass as a hare, or galloping across Midnight London in the stark light of the eternally full moon. It didn't help.

'Hoggins, why is everything colossally—' She stopped, frowning. 'Oh.'

The Hog was her just-possibly-magical pocket hedge-hog and adventure buddy. Or had been. It was hard to remember that he wasn't there anymore. No comforting warmth in her pocket. No grumbling grunts demanding worms. After a worrying period of being even more lazy and greedy than usual, in which she'd thought he might be ill, he had slipped into the deep sleep of hibernation. He was now tucked up in a bundle of warm leaves in his cardboard hog-palace, and she was hog-less (and banned from playing any loud music in her room until spring). Could her life get any worse?

She winced as a sound almost at the peak of human hearing echoed through the wall and made her book-shelves vibrate – the devil-baby, wailing like a foghorn being mugged by a car alarm. Why couldn't *he* hibernate until spring? She'd been kinda looking forward to being a sister, but it had been a lot better in theory. She'd picked him up once, and he'd erupted at both ends. She wasn't doing that again. As far as she could see, the only good thing about him was that the top of his head was super soft and smelt quite nice. Everything else was a hard 'no'.

Sleep was clearly going to be impossible. It wasn't just the baby howling, but the nasty twisting sense that some-thing was wrong and she couldn't fix it. She was also, she didn't want to admit to herself, waiting to hear the midnight chimes, like she did every night nowadays. With her window cracked open a little, you could make out the chimes of Big Ben drifting down the river. She wasn't sure why she did it, as they just made her feel worse. Like scratching the scab off a cut so it couldn't heal. For a brief moment though, it made her feel connected to her other home, knowing it was midnight in both places.

She edged closer to the window, despite the cold draught seeping under the curtain. As she did, the first haunting sound of the quarter bells, coming just before the real bongs, drifted to her on the breeze. She sang along under her breath, reciting the Night Folk rhyme that her friend Tarkus had taught her.

'All through this night, moon be my faith, and by its light, all shall be safe.'

The first bong came as the hammers fell on the enormous main bell, the true Big Ben, and it rang out in its unmistakable deep metallic voice. She was surprised to feel herself suppressing a sob, even though she totally wasn't a crier. Then . . . things got weird. The second bong started normally, then became a dragged out crawl of distorted noise, like someone slowing down a recording. All other sound stopped too. London's constant night-time drone of traffic faded away to nothing.

The silence was broken by the high-pitched screech of bicycle brakes, followed by glass-shattering levels of frantic banging. Someone, or something, was hammering on Emily's bedroom window!

CHAPTER 2

Heart pounding, Emily pulled the curtain back. She flinched as a white bird frantically flapped and scraped at the window. Wait, not a bird, a feathered hand! The owner of the hand was on a bike hovering in mid-air, with a shiny black umbrella clipped to its handle-bars. They had a black uniform with silver buttons, and a white-feathered, beaked face. It was Hunts-by-Night, the owl-lady from the Night Post.

'Helloooo!' she hooted happily, her hand still flapping for Emily to open the window.

'Oh my giddy aunt! Hunts-by-Night, hello!' Emily shouted, scrabbling to open the latch.

Hunts-by-Night hovered in the darkness on her gravity-defying bike, her white feathers tinted orange by the glare of the street lights. An eerie prickling passed over Emily's skin; magic. It came from the umbrella, a nightshade, made from pure midnight itself, allowing a small piece of the Midnight Hour's magic to be brought out into the Daylight world. It kept the post bike flying, and could stop time long enough to get deliveries done. Only it didn't look like Hunts-by-Night was here to deliver anything.

'Come, gather your things, yoooo must come with me, and we don't have long.' She beckoned Emily to join her.

'What? Where? How are you even here?'

'No time for chat, featherling. I'm not here, not officially, but the Midnight Hour needs yoooo.'

It was all Emily needed to hear. There was adventure afoot, and she could be part of it. She could be special again. Heart racing, and swallowing a hundred questions (with great difficulty as she was a very curious person), Emily dived off the bed to grab her things.

'Egglet, dressing less Daylight would be advisable.' The owl-lady's beak looked as frowny as a beak can. 'Things have changed, and not for the better.'

'But this is what I wear, errrm . . .' Emily dumped her comfort hoodie, and instead grabbed for her blackest clothes, channelling her inner goth. She matched her slightly-too-tight rock-star jeans with her velvet top with the weird lacy bit on, and shrugged into her mum's beloved black bomber jacket. She tugged on her particularly huge and offensive black boots (because big boots are best) and her flattest cap, then cast around for further inspiration. 'Ah hah!'

She grabbed the plastic fangtastic Dracula costume she'd been bodging together for Halloween (including glow-in-the-dark fangs, face paint and bin-bag cape) and stuffed it all into her ever-ready adventurer's bag. The one with the 'Hedgehog Friend' badge on the strap.

'Sorted.'

The owl eyed her up and down then shook her head (which was disconcerting, as she could turn it almost all the way round) but said nothing, so Emily figured she passed.

Emily cast a sad glance at the sprawling hog-palace as a vigorous snore vibrated the cardboard towers from within. 'Not this time, Hog. I'll be back soon though. I hope.'

The owl beckoned her again, feathered hand fluttering. 'Come, we must fly. The nightshade's magic will sooooon run out.'

'But I . . .' Emily shot a desperate glance at the door. 'I've got to tell Mum and Dad. It's not fair otherwise. Just give me a minute.'

'There is no minute to give. Yooo cannot leave the

frozen time field of the nightshade. If you step out, midnight will chime and yooo will be stranded here.'

Emily squirmed as the agony of it made her tummy roll. She couldn't miss this chance to get back in but—

'I don't want them to think I just ran off . . . not again.'

The owl glanced at the bike's handlebars and the brass timer that was busy ticking away there.

'There's no time.' The owl reached inside her jacket and, with a wince, pulled a long white feather out. She passed it to Emily.

'Here, fluff, this will help. Alan is a comrade-in-post. He will understand that I would not take yooo lightly.'

Emily placed the feather on her pillow, then, adventurer's bag over her shoulder, scrambled precariously out of the window. There was a moment of awful yawning vertigo as she looked down at the front garden below, but then she was in Hunts-by-Night's soft yet strong grip, and hoisted on to the empty parcel rack at the back. As they bobbed in mid-air, the owl-lady twisted around in her saddle, her head rotating much further than seemed natural. A feathery finger darted to her beak, and her thin black tongue licked something then pressed it to Emily's forehead. Emily reached up and her fingers felt a small piece of paper stuck there.

'What's that? Is it magic?'

'It's a stamp,' said Hunts-by-Night. 'Enough rules are

being broken already without transporting unstamped post.'

'Oh, okay,' said Emily.

As she turned away, the owl-lady's shoulders shook, in what looked suspiciously like laughter.

'Oi! Are you taking the mick?'

'Hoo hoo!' chuckled the owl.

Emily shook her head. *Owls, man. Weird sense of humour.*

The owl-lady gripped the handlebars and leant forward like a skier preparing for the off.

'Hold tight.'

Emily settled her feet securely on the frame then leant forward and gingerly held the owl-lady's tiny waist. She could feel the ghost softness of the feathers moving like silk under the stiff fabric of the Night Post jacket. Her tummy fizzed with excitement. There was a jingle and a jerk and the bike flung itself into the air, as if it had wings itself. Emily absolutely did not let out a muffled shriek.

They drifted down the street, over the rooftops of Emily's neighbours, the distant river a black mirror reflecting the lights of the city. The buildings before them formed a rolling terrain of tile-topped hills and glass-faced cliffs. The new perspective made her boring world suddenly enchanted. As soon as they were up, they were down again, landing by the ancient oak door in the wall of the churchyard. Emily's heart sank faster than the bike.

'We won't be able to get in. This is sealed.'

The owl made a chirruping *tch-tch* noise, which might have been a laugh. 'Not tonight it isn't. It's not what yooo know but whoo-ooo.'

In one smooth movement she closed the nightshade. As she did, there was a lurch in the world as time restarted and, as if Emily's ears had popped, all the sounds of London flooded back in. Emily could hear traffic and smell fumes and, in the distance, just make out the chimes of Big Ben tolling midnight.

'Quick,' Emily gasped, panic clawing at her. 'We don't have long.'

The owl rolled her eyes, which was a significant move considering the size of them. 'Would you teach your grand-sire to snatch field mice?'

She produced a large iron key from her top pocket and leant forward gracefully over the handlebars, stretching further than Emily could have, and slotted the key straight into the lock. The chimes continued, and Emily's grip on the tail of the owl's jacket grew tight.

'Please—'

'All is moss-lined and warm, fluff,' said the owl, turning the key and pushing the door open in a single smooth movement. With one kick of her foot they rolled through, just as the chimes finished ringing midnight.

They passed into the bright silvered gaze of the full moon and the welcome embrace of the Midnight Hour. Emily's whole body tingled as magic flowed over her like warm water. If the nightshade had been a trickle, this was a flood. Her other self, her Pooka self, stirred within. Her threefold forms scenting the night air, her mercurial wriggling luck suddenly vivid and alive inside her. She stretched and sighed with satisfaction. She was magic again, she was home. The thrill lasted only seconds before worries boiled up. Troublesome things were clearly happening here and, against all of her mum's adventuring rules, she was leaving home without either permission or her hedgehog. Worse, she'd done it knowingly under-snacked. It all felt wrong and she hoped it wasn't a bad omen.

They flew again, Midnight London beneath them now, glittering like an exotic beetle's casing. No street lights or over-lit buildings here, but instead the dance of gas lamps, flares of coloured magic, and the iridescence of flying folk. In the distance blazed the emerald arc-light candle that was the tower of Big Ben, the Great Working, the building-sized spell that held the whole Midnight Hour together. Emily let out a yelp of glee. Despite her worries, it was good being home.

They raced across London and Emily knew enough to

use the river and the fixed unmissable glow of the Great Working to track her progress. They were flying straight towards St Paul's Cathedral, which loomed over the offices of the Night Post, where her dad had been fired from. Behind the cathedral's dome, there was something huge and dark on the skyline that Emily hadn't seen before. She was trying to crane over the owl-lady's shoulder for a better look, when the bike suddenly dived and all Emily could do was hold on for dear life. She had witnessed some pretty dramatic skid landings by Hunts-by-Night in the past, but the bike barely made a sound as it touched down on the flat roof of the Night Post building. The owl-lady was in stealth mode. Hunts-by-Night craned her neck all the way around, searching every corner of the lead roof, before nodding.

'Now, featherling, we must be as silent as a moonlight hunter. You are not toooo be seen, or it will go ill for us both.'

She dismounted, and held the bike while Emily hauled herself off. She was stiff and the black jeans were definitely digging in. Cool did not equal comfortable, it seemed. The owl-lady strode over to the little shed-like structure that contained the access door to the stairs, and produced a large roll of colourful paper, a coil of ribbon, and some scissors.

'I left this in readiness. You must not be seen or we are

in big trouble.'

'What are you going to do with— Oh, no way. Absolutely not,' said Emily, backing away.

Minutes later, a very aggrieved voice rang out from within a tower of wrapping paper tied off with a scarlet bow.

'This is totally uncalled for.'

The owl-lady (who was *much* stronger than she looked) scooped Emily up effortlessly in both arms like a baby and carried her down through the Night Post building.

'Hush, yooo are a parcel. Parcels doo-oo not talk.' The owl hesitated – years of delivering for the Night Post had given her some insight into these things. 'Well, *most* parcels dooo not talk, and yooo are one of those. Hush now, this is the dangerous bit.'

They were soon surrounded by the loud buzz of manic activity. Emily had visited enough times with her dad that she could recognize the frantic chaos of the sorting room. Every sorcerously stamped packet and parcel in the Hour came through here. Emily was just poking a small hole in her wrappings to take a peek when an amplified voice boomed out over the chaos.

'YOU! Hold it right there, owl!'

CHAPTER 3

As the terrible shout echoed in the air, the whole sorting room stopped dead. An ear-grating noise followed, a clanking, puffing, chugging, rattling, steam whistle of a noise, and Emily felt the owl's muscles tense.

Through her peephole she saw a metal monstrosity roll into view. A brass wheelchair, with huge great chonking metal wheels at either side, seemingly more suited for a paddle steamer. Attached behind the chair was the towering boiler of a cacophonous steam engine, thick black smoke pouring from its chimney, and steam hissing from its pipes. In the chair, strapped in with ironwork, was a sagging dusty corpse in a cobweb-strewn Night Post uniform decorated with tarnished medals.

It was her old enemy, the Postmaster General! The horrible Dead man who ran the Night Post and hated her and all Day Folk. The last time she'd been here, he'd been stuffed away in a jar after his tattered corpse fell apart in a fit of apocalyptic rage. Her friend Japonica had been in charge, but now the Postmaster was back and, it seemed, worse than ever.

There was a pale movement at the front, and Emily shuddered to see that it was his all-too mobile severed hand, holding on to a brass steering lever like a great grey tarantula.

'You! Eats Mice or whatever your name is. Where have you been?' The Postmaster's screeching voice rattled out of a large speaking horn clamped to the side of the steam-chair. 'There are letters waiting for you!'

'I had an express delivery stamp, sir, and had to go,' the owl replied in calm tones, but Emily could feel her muscles were still clenched tight. The pale spider-hand twitched, and the steam-chair and its horrid passenger shot nearer. The movement made the body jerk in its metal straps, and dust sifted from it in a cloud.

'What's that you've got there?' The hand pointed a pallid finger at the parcel of Emily.

The owl shrugged. 'Just lost post. Its label has fallen off.

I am taking it to the lost-post rooo-hoom.'

A mouse poked out from the empty eye socket of the Postmaster to see what was going on.

'Just open it and see what's in it,' the Postmaster barked into the speaking horn. The hand flexed on the controls, and the engine revved as if eager to rip the parcel open. Emily had to suppress a gasp.

'*Sir!*' The owl sounded as shocked as if he'd told her not to eat shrews. 'That would break the sevenfold vow of postal defence that I, *that we*, took.'

She paused, then casually shook Emily, who nearly squealed. 'Plus, it might be full of mind-worms, it's certainly wriggly and heavy enough.'

Oi! thought Emily above the rising tide of terror. The owl shifted her stance and held the whole parcel out to the Postmaster. From this close, Emily could see the mice frolicking inside his head.

'Of course, if *yooo* want to open it . . . ?'

You have got to be kidding. Emily held her breath.

There was a pause. The hand balanced on its thumb and drummed its other fingers in thought. There was a giant clatter from behind them in the post room as something heavy threw itself off a shelf and started to eat the other post around it. The Postmaster twitched and jerked.

'No, no. Get rid of it and get back to work.' The hand was already groping for the brass lever to spin the chair.

'Firing all of those daysie-sympathizing traitors has left us short-handed.'

With that, the steam-chair hissed and roared, and he skidded away across the sorting room floor, yelling dire threats at the whole workforce.

The owl stood very still for a moment, then walked calmly out of the room through a little side door.

'Phew-ooh-hoo. That was close, my egglet.' She rounded a corner, then paused to stand Emily on her feet up against a wall. 'We're safe here, yooo can walk.'

Sharp talons ripped into the paper near her face, and she could breathe and see properly again. They were standing by a large scarred wooden door, reinforced with iron and covered in magical symbols. A brass plaque read, simply, 'Lost Post'. Hunts-by-Night cranked an iron handle and large cogs turned all around the door frame. It reminded Emily of a bank vault. When Hunts-by-Night heaved the door open, it was nearly a foot thick, built up of layers of oak and metal.

'Quickly, inside now, and keep your wits about you. The lost post has grown wild of late.'

'Ah-hurm!' Emily coughed. Her head was free but she was still wrapped up like a parcel, trapped by ribbons.

'Hoo-hoo!'

Owls, man. Jeez.

A slice of a knife-sharp talon freed her and they went

together into the darkened room, Hunts-by-Night dragging the vault door shut behind them.

'That is some security for a lost post room,' said Emily.

'More safety than security,' Hunts-by-Night said, her head now twisting all the way from side to side as she scanned the murky dark around them. 'Sometimes the post tries to escape.'

'What do you mean "escape"? It's just post, right?'

No one can do side-eye like an owl. Emily's hair nearly ignited under the scornful gaze cast her way.

'Yooo of all people should know that it's never "just post".'

She was right. That had been a doofus thing to say. The Night Post delivered to the strangest people, who received even stranger post. Her dad had been a Dangerous Deliveries Specialist, and often it was the package that was dangerous rather than the delivery. She'd seen parcels that hopped, crawled or glowed so bright you could see the bones in your hands. Who knew what was waiting in here?

It was very dark, except for the faint umber and purple glow of sorcery. All around them, the room hummed and buzzed and clicked and twittered and, worryingly, may well just have growled too. It made Emily think of a jungle at night, pulsing with unseen life and movement. Hunts-by-Night pulled a heavy lever on the wall, and as gas lamps lit up the room, Emily gasped.

An enormous landscape of post lay before her. Teetering mountains of poorly stacked parcels, brown paper and string sheered down into valleys full of smaller letters. Paths wound between them and over them, disappearing off into the hazy distance. Wait, distance?

'How big is this place?'

'No one knows anymore.' Hunts-by-Night was busying herself filling up two hand lanterns with oil. 'Much of the lost post was of a magical nature. Putting it all too-ooh-gether in one place . . .' She paused as a bright green light shone from the lanterns and made her eyes gleam. 'Well, such a concentration of magic has made conditions in here unu-oo-sual. It might be another dimension in its own right. Owls do not trouble themselves with such things though.'

'Wait, is this place actually dangerous?'

'Not according to management, no. None of the posties whooo've gone missing have ever registered an official health and safety complaint.'

'But, wait,' said Emily with her brow furrowed, 'how can they if they're missing?'

The owl raised one enormous eyebrow and said nothing. She handed Emily a lantern, then after one more careful scan of the area they stepped out on to a plain of flattened envelopes. The postal cliffs reared high above them.

'Come.'

'Where exactly are we going anyway? You still haven't told me what I'm doing here.'

'We're going where yooo need to be to dooo what you need to doo-hoo,' said the owl, and continued down the valley of parcels.

'Textbook enigmatic,' muttered Emily as she hiked. 'Love that. Never ends badly.'

Even for the Night Post, this post was weird, and the further they got from the door, the weirder it got. This post had aged, matured, *mulched*. The parcels were squooshed together, coruscating with the light of leaking magic like a covering of moss. Their contents tumbled out everywhere. Scarves and letters and mouldy chocolates, like any postbag, but also wands and orbs, stuffed salamanders and twining tentacles. Here and there she saw big rips and claw marks on empty crates that suggested things had actually let themselves out. It was a worry.

The letters underfoot deadened the sound of their steps like leaves on a forest floor, but all around were other noises, and glimpses of furtive movement in the shadows. The light from their lamps only lit up a small circle around them and all else was only magic phosphorescence, shadows and scurrying.

'There's loads of things around. I can smell 'em,' said

Emily, using her powerful Pooka nose.

'Oh, most probably,' said the owl. 'The post has been breeding and cross-breeding in here for centuries. There's all sorts.'

'Well, what should we do?'

'Try not to look like prey.'

Emily proffered a look to the heavens. 'How does this sort of thing keep happening to me? I mainly just want to eat biscuits and occasionally turn into a pony. Is that too much to ask?'

The door had long since vanished behind them and Emily had no idea where they were. Looking up, she saw a flock of magic books turning and circling to land on the slopes above them. She smiled, comforted to see something familiar in such a strange place. The flying books of the Midnight Hour were one of her favourite things. She'd often go for a stroll through Paternoster Row, where they all roosted, to feed them some comma crumbs. She was about to click her tongue and whistle these ones down when she noticed how leathery and warty their covers were, and how sharp and nasty the edges of their bindings looked. A small glowing lizard scurried across a nearby post pile and the flock swooped down, landing on it in a dense clump of rustling paper and swiftly ended high-pitched squeals. Apparently they were bad books. One-star reviews all round. Emily walked faster to be closer to Hunts-by-Night.

After another endless series of turns and a nasty near-miss with something that looked like a cross between a scorpion, a rhino and a toast rack, they headed down a narrow incline. At the brown-papered bottom was a massive engraved pillar with a broken statue atop it. Only its two huge legs were left, leaving it looking like a monument to a pair of trousers. The owl looked carefully behind them then did her double nod.

'Despair,' she said to Emily, who was loitering at the base of the pillar.

'Eh?'

'Despair. Press where it says "despair" on the pillar.'

'Oh right, hang on.' She trailed a finger over the stone, finding it difficult to read the moss-filled words in the poor light. '"Look on my works, ye mighty, and" – ah hah! – "*Despair*"!'

She pressed the carving and there was a clunk as the word moved back, and then the rickety-click of clockwork winding. One of the vast legs above kicked out like a cancan dancer, and a portion of the pillar slid open, revealing a stairway within. They lit the way down the spiral stairs with their lamps, until they reached another open doorway. Beyond it was a flickering light. As they stepped out, blinking, into a fire-lit clearing, a loud, posh, and very familiar voice said,

'Ah, there you are! About time too.'

CHAPTER 4

'Japonica!' Emily said joyfully.

The secret passage had brought them out into a hidden clearing in the postal jungle. In the middle, next to a bright burning campfire of parcels, stood one of Emily's dearest friends in the Hour – Japonica Rhowse, recently deposed head honcho of the Night Post, daemoness, and increasingly snappy dresser. She was wearing a khaki safari suit, long shorts with many stitched-on pockets, and a tall pith helmet. Her obsidian skin reflected the firelight but didn't gleam as brightly as her ruby-red eyes. Her fang-filled mouth split into a huge grin.

'Come along then. I'm just making tea.'

Japonica lifted a large steaming camp kettle from where it dangled on a tripod over the fire. The fire was the centre point of a small encampment of large, robust canvas structures – more huts than tents – some rigged out as homes, one as a kitchen, and another full of flying post bikes, a rack of nightshades and other oddments. Around the fire were a number of other familiar faces, posties Emily knew were friends of her dad, a number of goats, and, so big he took up a whole seating log himself . . . 'Jonesy!'

Emily ran over to the huge post troll and he gave her a big hug. 'You brought the whole family too.' Emily doffed her flat cap at the goats, as she knew was only polite. They all nodded and bleated back.

'Aye, Miss Emily. Felt safer in here it did.'

Emily looked at the darkness outside the ring of the campfire's light, a darkness full of glinting eyes and teeth (or whatever weird magic things had in place of teeth, probably suckers or something).

'Yeah, sure. Just how bad have things got?'

'Oh quite, quite bad,' said Japonica cheerfully. 'However, I must insist we have tea and cake before discussing imminent doom.'

'You've got cake?' said Emily. 'Here?'

'Of course, dear. Certain standards must be maintained.'

Things did feel a bit less stressful after tea in bone-china cups and cake on delicate plates by the fireside.

Hunts-by-Night had passed on cake but had been delighted when Japonica produced a dormouse in aspic. They all perched on logs and the fire made things cosy despite the distant screeches and howls from the darkness beyond. Japonica threw another parcel on the flames, and it roared up in a purple haze.

'There, isn't that better?'

'Yup,' said Emily, and masked a burp with her hand. 'Now, will someone please tell me what's going on? Ideally in some detail, and with minimum use of enigma, allusion, or statements like "you'll know when the time is right". Go.' She pointed a still-slightly-jammy finger at Japonica. 'Start with why we're in the mail-fail jungle.' She leant in closer to say in low tones, 'Oh, and magnificent shorts, by the way. Big thumbs-up.'

'Thank you,' mouthed Japonica, then, in louder tones, 'There has been some unpleasantness. Not just within the Night Post, but across our midnight realm.' She gestured at Emily. 'Ever since you saved the Great Working things have been greatly amiss with the spell. The time shadows have led to much unrest.'

Japonica was talking about when Emily had narrowly managed to stop the evil plans of the Nocturne, her actual honest-to-god nemesis (and who had one of them at her age?). But what on earth was a time shadow? She was about to ask but Japonica pressed on.

'A new anti-Daylight party of the Dead has risen to power in parliament on the back of this fear. The MBDA. It stands for their mission – Make Britain Dark Again.'

Jonesy growled as she spoke, his tusks vibrating. The goats bleated angry agreement.

'Quite, Jones family. Quite,' said Japonica.

'I thought the Dead had always been anti-Daylight?' said Emily. 'All the ones who've tried to eat me have been anyway.'

'This is different,' said Japonica, shaking her head. 'Now they talk of the Daylight as an enemy, not somewhere we left because there wasn't enough magic for us to stay.' Japonica scowled, all of her fangs glinting as she did. 'Their horrible doctrine has spread like wildfire amongst the small-minded and easily gulled. Tempers are high, fingers have been pointed –' she cocked a thumb at herself – 'all Daylight sympathizers driven out of work. And here we are.'

She gestured around, back to her usual fiercely chipper self. Emily chewed her lip. It was a lot to take in.

'But why are you hiding in the lost-post room?'

'Well,' said Japonica, 'there was also the small matter of some spurious charges relating to the false imprisonment of a member of the Dead, and a superior officer.' Japonica studiously examined her fingernails as she spoke. Emily grinned, knowing it had been her friend who had put the

Postmaster in a jar then 'forgotten' about him.

'I have hidden here, in the last place they'd look. Others who have been unfairly victimized have taken shelter here too.'

There was a low rumbling from the other posties on the far side of the fire. They bit their lips and nodded their heads, faces tight with anger and sorrow.

'Others, brave others,' she nodded here at Hunts-by-Night, 'stay within the service to keep us informed and work in secret to further our agenda.'

Emily, whose head was spinning a bit, raised a hand. 'Right, okay, not bad for a change, I got most of that. New bad people in charge, kicking out Daylight-friendly types from jobs, sacking and evicting my dad.' She leant forward, her brow furrowed. 'But what I don't get is what you're doing now and why I'm here?'

'What are we doing?' said Japonica. 'Why, we're the Resistance, darling, and we need your help.'

'Riiiight, and what will I be resisting, specifically?'

'Well, we're mainly resisting their plans to turn off the Great Working, destroy the Midnight Hour, and conquer the Daylight by making it dark for ever.' Japonica smiled encouragingly. 'We thought you'd probably like to help.'

There was a stunned silence from Emily, broken only by the sound of her jaw hitting the floor.

'Whuh?' she said, intelligently.

'Did I not mention that at the start?' said Japonica, brightly. 'That's the whole "Make Britain Dark Again" bit. Sorry, thought that was obvious from context.'

'No,' said Emily, 'that wasn't completely clear, no.'

'Ah,' Japonica nodded, lips pursed. 'Right, sorry, so yes, end of the Hour as we know it, shortly followed by the end of your world too, and you're here because our leader—'

'Wait,' interrupted Emily, 'you're not in charge?'

'No, dear, only of the postal division. We've got a visionary tactical genius in charge and he felt very strongly that you could be the key to our battle plans.'

'I know I say this a lot, but – and I really mean this wholeheartedly,' said Emily, ' – *why me?*'

'Because,' said an oddly familiar voice from the shadows, 'the Resistance needs a giant gob to speak truth to Powers.'

Striding out from the secret entrance came a tall figure sporting a black top hat, smoked eyeglasses, a huge bushy beard, and a long black leather coat. He addressed the Resistance group. 'Sorry I'm late, they've doubled the sentries again.' He turned back to Emily. 'You've normally been sarcastic by now, are you completely well?'

The accent was familiar but not the appearance. Only as he pulled off the dark glasses and the flickering yellow flame of his eyes spilt out, alongside a sudden scent of jasmine, did she know him.

'Tarkus?'

He inclined his head in reply.

'Have you got the big fake beard as a disguise to cover your sad moustache?' she said.

Tarkus Poswa, ghûl, Probationary Inspector of the Night Watch, and long-suffering adventure buddy of a Pooka disaster vortex, fingered his big and increasingly obviously fake beard.

'This is a necessary disguise. I'm a wanted ghûl.' He scowled. 'And my moustache is not sad.'

He grinned suddenly, his white teeth visible through the undergrowth of his big stick-on beard. 'It's good to see you, Librarian.'

She ran over to him, stopped (he wasn't much for being hugged), gave him a fond look, and punched him in the arm instead. The distinct floral smell of his scent magic wafted out of his coat as she did.

'You too, Inspector.'

'Ah, alas, inspector no more. My stellar career arc has been arrested.' He frowned. 'Which is also what I'll be if they ever get hold of me.'

He sat down heavily on a fireside log and reached behind his pointy ears to unclip his beard with a sigh of relief. Now Emily could see his whole face, he looked strained and thin. His usually clear brown skin was edging into green.

'What? Really? But you love being a Night Watchman.'

'Alas, the Watch no longer loves me. They have purged

their ranks of any Daylight sympathizers.' Tarkus nodded his head towards her. 'After the last few chaotic nightmares you've involved me in, I definitely qualified.'

'Adventures,' said Emily firmly. 'Not chaotic nightmares – *adventures*. We're adventure buddies.'

'Hrrrrm,' said Tarkus, his hand rubbing his once-fractured ribs. 'Well, however you phrase it, I'm out on my ear.'

'That's rotten,' she said, and meant it. 'But why do they want to arrest you?'

'Possibly because I forgot to hand something back in when I was given my marching orders,' said Tarkus with a grin that crossed from sheepish to sly in rapid succession. 'They took everything else, badge, truncheon and whistle, but . . .'

From a pocket in his very manly leather coat he produced an object that filled his palm with the green light of sorcery.

'Ooh, the Master Key!' said Emily.

The key was a part of the master spell, the Great Working, that held the Midnight Hour outside of time. It had been issued to Tarkus during his brief reign as Provisional Inspector in charge of Doors, Portals, Gates and other Means of Egress (or was it egrets? She always got that mixed up) and was very powerful. It could open any door, including ones to the Daylight world.

'Good job too, or you'd still be stuck outside.' He looked wistful. 'I really miss that whistle though. I paid for it with my own money.'

Emily grinned. 'Why, Tarkus Poswa, I'd never have had you down for light fingers. You've changed.'

'I've had to.' His expression hardened. 'If they do break the Great Working, my family and all the other magically reliant folk like them simply won't survive.'

There was a grim ripple of growls and mutters from around the fire as he spoke. Any cosiness Emily had felt vanished.

'I just don't get it,' she said. 'How have things gone so bad so quickly?'

'It was the time shadows. Since they started appearing –' he shook his head – 'people have been scared, and this MBDA hate has spread like a sickness.'

'What are these blinking time shadows?' said Emily.

'Honestly, it will be easier to show you.'

He stood up suddenly, pocketing the key. 'So, enough chat, we need to move.'

He cast his gaze around the camp. 'Friends, hopefully Miss Featherhaugh can deliver what we need. In the meantime, spread the word to the faithful. They'll be needed soon.'

He inclined his head courteously to Japonica.

'Miss Rhowse, I leave the command with you.'

Emily cleared her throat. Loudly. Everyone turned to look at her.

'Right, obviously I'll help, despite, as previously noted

many times, being far too young for this, and having strong reservations about the patriarchal oppression inherent in your use of "Miss". She was gabbling, that happened when things were tricksy. 'But, coupla things, I can't think why you'd need me when you're surrounded by brave magic types, and more importantly,' she leant in and grabbed Tarkus's sleeve, 'where's the blooming Library in all this? She's a semi-omnipotent demigod and a bit MI5. Hour-ending threats are what she's all about.'

Emily stalked around a bit, doing her best Library impression. 'She's always, "Oh, there is doom-doom, Emily, you must risk your lithe young form and excellent haircut to save us." . . .'

She trailed off, running out of breath.

'So why isn't she sorting this out? Because it sounds like her and Art could fix it by snapping their fingers.'

She snapped a finger herself to demonstrate. Japonica and Tarkus exchanged glances.

'That's just it, dear,' said Japonica. 'That's why we need you. The Library and Art have vanished.'

Tarkus continued. 'They're both missing. No one can find them.' He grasped her arm, his scent now that of sharp citrus. 'You're the only person I know who they are close to. You've got to help us find them or we're doomed.'

Emily nodded slowly.

'Oh, yeah, you sound just like her.'

CHAPTER 5

With a rattle, a clank, and a blood-chilling scream of terror, Emily cannoned out of a rusty iron chute on to a mouldy old mattress in a dingy back alley. She made a landing that was less cat-like and more a flailing octopus belly flop, which springboarded her off the mattress and into a heap on the dirty alley floor.

Tarkus popped out neatly after her, stepped over her crumpled form with a sigh, and concealed himself in the shadows to scout for trouble.

'The next time you push a girl into a haunted magical zero-gravity postal doom tube,' said Emily, sitting up and pulling something unidentifiable out of her hair with a shudder, 'give her a bit of warning first!'

'Right,' said Tarkus, completely ignoring her and pulling his enormous beard out of his pocket. 'You need to get the rest of your disguise on. The streets aren't safe anymore.'

'They never were,' muttered Emily, who had nearly been eaten here a non-insignificant number of times now. Before they had entered the tube, she had applied a layer of white face paint and thick black eyeshadow. A lot of eyeshadow. Now, she dug in her bag and produced her bin-bag cape and fake fangs.

'*That's* your disguise?' said Tarkus in arch tones.

'YES!' said Emily, jamming her fangs in and swooshing her cape around her shoulders.

'I vant to dwink your bluuurd,' she said draculamatically.

'Please don't, that's really quite uninformed and offensive,' said Tarkus, pinching the bridge of his nose.

'Well that rotten vampire Peregrine *did* want to drink my blood!'

'I wonder what could possibly have driven him to that, hmmm?'

She stuck her tongue out at him, causing her fangs to pop out and land on the disgusting floor.

'Nooooo!'

'Oh, sweet Hecate,' he muttered. 'I'd forgotten quite how painful this was.'

'Less of it, beardy – your disguise isn't much better,' she

said, as she wiped her fangs clean on her jeans. 'If you'd have said, I'd have bought some guinea pigs to stick to my chin too.'

He studied her, eyes lidded and face set. 'If your intention was to assemble a likeness of a vampiric panda, then I'd say you'd done well. As it is . . .' He reached forward and yanked her cap all the way down to her nose.

'Oi!'

'Keep your hat down, and your shiny collar up. And in the name of all that is unholy, if we're stopped, just for once in your entire life, let me do the talking.' He didn't look like he was joking.

'*Fine*. Whatevs. So, what now?' she said.

'I was hoping you'd tell me. You're the expert. We need to find the Library or Art as fast as possible.'

'Errrm . . . expert might be pushing it. Let me think. You've looked in the British Museum Reading Room?'

'Obviously.'

'Paternoster Row?'

'Of course.'

'Written her a letter?'

'I'm not an idiot.'

'Many would beg to differ. I'm one of them.' She bit her knuckle in thought. 'What about Art? Knocked on a painting?'

'The whole National Gallery. I was asked to leave in the end.'

'Hmmmmm.'

She paced around a bit, sucking her fangs in and out with a disgusting noise.

'Must you?'

'Helps me fink,' she lisped over the plastic. 'Ha! Got it!' she shouted, suddenly loud in the quiet of the alley, making him jump and clutch his beard.

'I've got special Librarian privileges. The Library always gets in touch through the Library card.' She was rooting through her bag. 'Well, one time she did anyway. Ah, here it is.' She brandished the thick piece of card that proclaimed her a Librarian. (Like being a postman, the job was a bit different here. She was basically a secret agent. Licence to shush.)

'So it stands to reason I can contact her on it. Pen.' She snapped her fingers.

Tarkus scowled. 'I'm the leader of the Resistance, not your assistant, you know?'

'If telling yourself that helps, Moneypenny, then you carry on.'

He handed over a cigar-sized brass fountain pen that was heavy enough to have doubled as a truncheon, and she leant on her bag to write on the card.

Hey Booky, it's me, Emily. Things are real bad and doom and stuff and I need to know where you

are ASAP. (That means As Soon As Possible if you haven't invented it yet.) Please please very important. Hope you're not on holiday.
Love and stuff, E x

There was a sigh so great and weighty behind her that she actually felt the breeze. It smelt of tarragon. 'That's honestly what you're putting?'

'What's wrong with that? Friendly, but gets to the point.'

'I cannot even— Never mind. How long will this take?'

She looked at the card, which sat unchanged. 'No idea, sorry. Never done it this way before.'

'Then we should get off the street. It's not safe to be out. I'll get us a ride.' He placed both index fingers in his mouth and blew a piercing whistle. Emily winced at the noise.

'What's that meant to do?'

'You'll see,' he said, looking rather too pleased with himself. All this 'in charge of the mysterious Resistance' thing was definitely going to his head. In the distance there was an answering whinny and then a clip-clop of hooves which grew louder and closer until a shimmering black-and-white shape cantered to a stop in front of Tarkus.

'Ink horse!' shouted Emily in excitement. This was Art's horse, or a horse created by Art anyway. She had once ridden out of one of Emily's mum's drawings on the back of it. The ink horse was made up of strokes of ink and the translucent white of paper, but was full-sized and really there. She nickered agreeably at Emily before turning back to bunt Tarkus in the arm with her head, making him stagger.

'Steady there, Painty,' said Tarkus, patting her nose as he smiled.

'Painty? That's what you went with?' said Emily. 'She's not even drawn with—'

'Shush,' said Tarkus very firmly over the top of her. 'I'll tell you what, the next time you get left with a magical art-based animal to look after because everybody else has wandered off, you can choose its name.' He glared at her, but Painty attempting to put her entire head under his arm made him smile again. He groped in his pocket and pulled out several small squares of paper. Holding his hand as flat as he could make it, he offered them to Painty, whose black tongue and big white teeth soon gobbled them up.

'What was that?'

'Drawings of sugar cubes. She loves them.'

He patted Painty's flank as she chewed contentedly. 'Come on, we'll have to walk for a bit before it's safe to ride.'

They emerged on the east side of St Paul's. Tarkus stopped and pointed into the distance.

'Here, look upon the time shadows that visit such fear upon the city.'

From their raised position by the cathedral, Emily could see far out across the east of the city. In this time, the buildings were still low enough not to block the view. High above the stonework, chimneys and low-flying witches, great dark shadowy shapes loomed above the city. They were vaster than anything else here, even dwarfing the huge cathedral behind them. Straight ahead was a time shadow so tall that she couldn't look up at it without craning her neck. It must have been the darkened form she'd glimpsed on her flight in. It was the oddest bloated shape, like a giant sausage that'd been squeezed at one end. It was covered with angular gleaming scales, and the whole thing flickered in and out of existence. Sometimes there, sometimes just a shadow. It was like a juddering old piece of black-and-white film reel, and it made Emily blink.

Across the other side of the river was another, this one so vast it even towered over the giant sausage thing. No curves here – this was a thin pyramidal structure that reached for the sky with glittering malice. It was about as 'dark lord' style a tower as you could get, and was lacking only a flaming eye at the top and an aggrieved owner in search of missing magical jewellery. It too flickered in that strange way, sometimes disappearing from existence altogether. Both of the enormous time shadows were truly terrifying to behold.

If you didn't know what they were, anyway.

'Dude, these aren't magical doom phenomena,' said Emily, pointing at them herself now. 'That's the Gherkin. That's the Shard.' She shook her head with confusion. 'They're just buildings from my time somehow showing through here.'

'The Resistance is aware of that, but hardly anyone else is,' Tarkus said. 'We have posties who recognize the shadows for what they really are but, to the normal folk of this city, they are terrible omens of invasion or worse.'

He scowled.

'There are more, they spring up everywhere throughout the city, swaying in and out of existence. Perhaps the worst of all is –' he pointed down the river to a giant yet lower-lying structure – 'Tower Bridge.'

'What's wrong with Tower Bridge?'

'We didn't have one! It wasn't built when the Hour was sealed and yet it's appeared. Well, sometimes.' He grimaced. 'Sometimes it's solid enough to walk across, then it flickers and gusts and is gone again.'

'I get how the big ones are scary, but like, free bridge – bonus, surely?'

He shook his head disapprovingly. 'Bridges shouldn't be occasional. There have been a number of unfortunate incidents.'

'Ah.'

'It's clear that time is leaking in, which means the Great

Working is failing.' Tarkus looked absolutely stone-faced. 'It is scaring people, at the exact same time these Make Britain Dark Again idiots are raising support to tear the Great Working down. I—'

'Who you callin' an idiot?'

A harsh voice interrupted Tarkus. It came from the hulking shape of a huge woman moving towards them. Her upper half was the size of a brewery barrel, solid flesh and muscle squeezed into a black lace dress that creaked at the seams, topped by a huge square head, under a big bonnet, joined to the shoulders without apparent benefit of a neck. Her bottom half, appearing from under her dress, was a writhing mass of thick grey tentacles, wider than Emily in some cases. Pinned to the front of her dress was a colossal red rosette with 'MBDA' in bold lettering in the middle.

Great.

'I said—'

'I heard you, madam,' said Tarkus calmly, 'but you must be mistaken, I didn't call anyone an idiot, I in fact—'

'You shut up.' The she-squid's tentacles thrashed and propelled her sinuously towards them. 'I know what I 'eard, and you ain't got no call to be talkin' about the people who are makin' this place better—' She stopped and leant around Tarkus to glare at Emily. 'What is *that*?'

Don't talk, don't talk, don't talk.

'That, madam, is a poor disfigured vampiric child, totally unable to speak, that I am taking to the—'

'You shut up, I said!' The she-squid's mouth opened wide; it went all the way across her head and was filled with teeth like broken glass. A thick tentacle rose up in front of Tarkus now, and hovered menacingly.

She slid sideways past Painty and her eyes bulged out of her grey-toned face as she stared at Emily.

Don't talk, don't talk.

'You. Where you from?'

Well, if she was going to ask questions, that was totally different, right?

'Landahn,' Emily said, in a bid to sound more convincingly urchin-like.

'You know what I mean.' The she-squid's grey face was flooding with a darker colour, like spilt ink. 'Where you *really* from?'

'Lambeth?' Emily ventured, and her fangs slid out of her mouth as she did. 'Oops.'

From the corner of her eye, she could see Tarkus wince and start reaching under his coat for weapons.

'Lookit you! Blinkin' daysie, I knew it! Disgustin' it is.'

The she-squid spat on the floor, and the stones fizzed with her burning spittle. 'Just you wait until we get that clock spell turned off. We'll give you what for then!'

She swelled as she shouted, her face all blue with ink,

and her tentacles writhing. She was working up to doing something bad.

To Emily's horror, the gob propelled her forward, and spoke for her.

'I'm from London. *Both* Londons.' She looked up at the towering she-squid. 'And do you know what else I am, you horrible woman?'

'What?' the she-squid said, her tentacles poised to strike.

Emily tensed and did something Mammy Espeth had been teaching her. She let a tiny bit of her Pooka self out. Just a little bit of hound to sniff out any weird magic. It also had the interesting side effect of making her eyes glow bright red.

'I'm a Pooka.'

The scarlet light of her eyes glinted off the ink-dark face in front of her, and she grinned with teeth that were more pointed than before.

'So how many years' bad luck would you like? Let me start counting. One?'

She poked the squid in her enormous chest, which was like poking, well, a massive wobbly squid.

The squid-lady paled as she looked down at the tiny finger. 'Two?'

Emily poked her again and this time she slithered back.

'Three?' She raised her hand, but the she-squid deflated

and slithered away, screeching and rubbing frantically at herself to rub the bad luck off.

Emily released the little bit of hound she'd seized hold of, and flicked back to normal. It was nowhere near as hard as a full change, but still made her feel a bit woozy. It didn't matter though, as the giggles overwhelmed the discomfort.

'Hoo hoo! Did you see her face?'

There was the sound of a slow clapping and she turned to see Tarkus leaning against Painty, applauding but not smiling.

'What's up with you? That was brilliant.'

'It was, you are brave, although, currently, I'd not be so fast to name myself Pooka in public.' He raised a hand before she could object. 'Anyway, that's not what bothers me.'

He frowned and stared after the squid-lady, now long gone, presumably home to touch wood and buy as many rabbit's feet as she could.

'This is exactly the new kind of awful that we are living with. Open intolerance on the street, and the Midnight Hour falling to pieces. We must find the Library before it all crumbles.'

Emily shook her head.

'Honestly, I've been coming here for, like, what? A year and a half? And you've had three universe-ending dilemmas in that time. What did you do without me?'

'It is precisely the other way around.' Tarkus tutted. 'Since you arrived, dilemmas directly linked to you have been occurring.'

'Oh, hold on, mister. You're not pinning it on me. You've got big problems and I fix 'em. I should get a statue.'

'You should get a bill.' He looked pointedly at her. 'Who brought the bad pennies back in and started this whole carry-on?'

'That is totally unfair. No one told me they were— In fact, no one tells me anything! The constant theme here is people not telling me things I need to know.' She waved her all-powerful and very intimidating finger at him. 'Your take-home is to tell the heroic girl all the facts at the start!'

'Hrrrrm,' Tarkus harrumphed.

Emily narrowed her eyes in suspicion. 'On that topic, have you told me everything this time?'

'I'm just thinking, let me see . . .' He counted the facts off on his fingers as he did. 'Threat to fabric of world from MBDA, Older Powers missing, time shadows.' He gestured vaguely at her. 'Enormously annoying disaster nexus . . .'

'Oi!'

He flinched, but not at her outburst.

'Oh, actually, there is something I should have mentioned . . . the Hunt.'

As he spoke, there was the distant sound of a horn

blowing a long wailing cry, followed by a strange roaring. Tarkus's eyes went wide.

'*The Hunt!*'

'Yes, I heard you. What is it?'

He grabbed her arm and pulled her down the street.

'No time, they're coming!' he gasped as he ran.

'This is exactly what I'm talking about!'

CHAPTER 6

Tarkus dragged her along the street, panting and frantic, teeth sunk into his lower lip with worry. Painty clattered beside them, nostrils wide with panic. Behind them the awful sound of the hunting horn shrieked again, a tortured note that jangled Emily's nerves.

'Stop dragging me,' she gasped out. 'Get on Painty and I'll change. We can go much faster then.'

She pulled her arm from his grasp, and prepared to summon a Pooka form. He turned on her, as scared as she'd ever seen him.

'No, we can't! Running's the worst thing we could do.

That's how they get you. We've got to find— Ah! Thank Hecate!'

Tarkus ran to an iron-barred gate at the entrance to a tunnel-like alley between two buildings. He was already jamming his glowing Master Key into it before Emily had caught up. The lock gave with a click, and he wrenched the gate open with a squeal of rusty hinges.

'In! Now. Come on, Painty, you too. We can't be on the street.' He was practically vibrating as he ushered them through and locked the gate behind them. Emily's neck prickled with fear – she'd never seen him like this before. The street echoed with the angry brass of the horn, now mixed with strange rattling calls and the shouts and bellows of eager bloodlust, growing ever closer.

'What's going on? What's chasing—'

'There's no time!' His face was wild with panic, visible even behind his big fake beard. 'We need to be silent, and as far from the gate as we can.'

The alley was a dead end, full of foul-smelling rubbish and abandoned junk. They pressed themselves into the furthest corner to hide, as best as they could with a full-sized horse crammed in with them.

'Okay, okay,' Tarkus muttered and took a deep breath, then looked up, suddenly calm. 'Now.'

He raised a hand and his eyes flared, yellow flames licking around the edges of his dark glasses and illuminating the alley. He moved his hand around them in a wide circle and the stink levels from the grot on the floor rose sharply. Emily gagged, while Painty whinnied in alarm. Tarkus turned and thrust his arm forward towards the gate, and the stinking cloud of alley smell moved from them, forming an almost visible cloud of stench at the entrance. The area they were in suddenly smelt of, well, nothing at all. The sound of the Hunt grew closer.

'What now?' whispered Emily.

'Now, we pray the scent cloud will be enough to hide us,' said Tarkus, and crouched down in the shadows. He held his big black coat open like bat wings, and nodded Emily inside. She crouched with him, and he draped it over them both. Beside them, she could see that Painty had turned completely inky, her white glow vanishing so the horse was almost invisible in the half-light. Pressed as close to him as she'd ever been, Emily could feel Tarkus trembling, and the smell of leather mingled with the acidic scent of apples turning to vinegar. She tried not to think about how stuck in this alley they were if whatever Tarkus had done didn't work.

The terrible blasting of the demon horn was right on them now. There was a thumping of heavy steps and an odd scritch-scratch noise accompanying them. There was also a softer pitter-patter of smaller noises in between them, like a rain of frogs. Peeking through the coat, Emily could see the foggy street through the iron bars of the gate, and it was suddenly full of movement.

There were small white . . . somethings scurrying across the cobbles, running on four – or was it five? – legs. Like pale spiders, but with a thick, pronounced back and no head. Some of them climbed up the iron bars of the gate, and Emily tensed before they dropped off and scurried out of sight. Then the awful scratching noise got louder as the rest of the pack came into view. They were much larger versions of the scurrying headless spiders, hefty as Rottweilers. Dreadful pallid things with multi-jointed limbs. The awful scratching came from the huge pointed talons on the end of their legs. The pack halted for a moment, as if sensing their prey was near, and a particularly huge one stopped right in front of the alley gate.

In that moment, Emily's brain clicked and she could see what they were – they were *HANDS*. Giant severed hands, running on their claw-like fingernails. The huge ones must have been from ogres and giants, the tarantula-sized scouts from 'normal' Night Folk. The street outside was full of hunting hands, and she'd never been as scared in her life. She whimpered just once, and the huge hand outside twitched, then started to cast around, using its clawed index finger like an insect would use antennae. It scraped its jagged nail down one of the iron bars of the gate, then pushed at the lock. The iron groaned under its weight.

Tarkus gripped her arm so tight it hurt, and she froze, not even daring to breathe. It seemed impossible it wouldn't hear her heart as it hammered in her chest.

Then there was a shrieking blast on a bugle, and the pale hand stiffened, then spun around with a terrible fluid speed and bounded forward. The rest of the pack scuttled along behind it and in moments they were gone.

Emily sagged with relief inside the hot cave of Tarkus's coat, but he tightened his grip again, pressing a finger firmly to his lips. As he did, there was another noise from the fog, not thuds now, but friction, like shingle moved by violent waves on a beach. The noise reached a pitch, and then a black flurry passed the gateway at speed. It was so huge it blotted out the whole entrance, leaving only an impression of black slick scales. After it, another, and another, further out in the street, but so big and moving so fast that Emily could just catch a nightmare glimpse of vast sinuous creatures, like racing snakes the size of a train – *wyrms*. They had saddles and riders on their backs wearing armour of black and the bloodiest of reds, topped with glittering gold-visored helmets decked with dark plumes.

For a fraction of a moment, Emily's Pooka nose picked up something from the Hunt, a smell of something old and dry and Dead. A scent she could almost recognize . . . but then it and they were gone. The rasping of the wyrms' scaled bellies rubbing on the cobbles echoed behind them, there was another blast of the shrieking horn, then all was quiet again. Emily and Tarkus let out a combined breath and slumped against each other, without caring what grimy filth they were sitting in.

'Let us never do that again,' said Tarkus.

'Agreed,' said Emily, who just for once hadn't got a single funny thing to add. All she could imagine were those awful spider hands crawling over her. This chain of thought was thankfully broken by Painty, who, apparently feeling left out, jammed her head in between them and licked their ears.

'Argh, get off!'

They were back on the street, but everything was different. Having moonlit Victorian London around her normally made Emily's heart sing, but now, with the awful prospect of the hellish Hunt possibly lurking around any corner, she felt like prey. Hunted. She shivered and pulled her bin-bag cape right up to eye-shadow level. Tarkus was ahead with Painty, gaze alert and questing as he led them along at a pace. 'But not too fast,' as he'd insisted. 'We don't want to look like we're running away.'

She drew level with him.

'So what the hell was that?' she said in a hoarse whisper.

'That was the Hunt.'

'I figured that. Handsy, slithery terror, got it.' She narrowed her eyes. 'But where did they come from? What did they want?'

'Oh, they're out here to keep us safe,' he said, and smiled a thin smile that never reached his eyes.

'Safe from what?'

He sighed.

'You know, threats to the realm, like people from the Daylight, or Pooka.'

'What!' Emily half yelled, before clapping her hand to her mouth as he glared at her. They were moving through busier streets now, with a few Night Folk shambling about. Heads had turned at Emily's shout and Tarkus hurried her along around a corner. He moved closer and talked in low tones.

'The MBDA – the idiots we were talking about earlier – have convinced people that all these time shadows, the future leaking in, is actually a plot. That the Day Folk and the Pooka are behind it all.'

Emily's mouth dropped open at the colossal injustice of this. The time shadows were a mystery, not a conspiracy, and the Pooka were definitely completely innocent. For once.

'But they—'

Tarkus raised a hand to stop her before her volume level could go up any more.

'I know, I know. They just needed someone to blame, and you are it.' He rubbed at his temple, eyes screwed shut. 'And so now the Hunt roams the streets looking for any offenders. In fact, it was likely your little display earlier that got them called out.'

He raised his hand even higher as her gob prepared to launch.

'And you are completely right, I should have told you earlier. I'm sorry, I've just got a lot of other terrible things going round in my head at present.'

For a moment, even through the fake beard and the circles of smoked glass covering his flaming eyes, he looked terribly young.

'Oh Tarkus, this is horrible.' Her heart gave a lurch as she thought of her Pooka family. 'Is . . . are . . . Do you know if Mammy and the clan are okay?'

He gave a pinched little helpless smile and shook his head. 'I honestly don't know. I haven't heard anything from them recently.'

Her stomach rolled and she thought there was a good chance she was going to be sick.

'Oh god, we need to . . .' She honestly didn't know what they needed to do. A warm hand rested on her shoulder then, and she looked up gratefully as Tarkus squeezed it just the once. She was surprised – he was not big on PDA. Or indeed any displays of affection, let alone public ones.

She figured it was something to do with being ghûl – he was probably emitting most of his emotions by smell or something.

'I know,' he said. 'It's all wrong, and we'll put it right. But first we need to get off the street.'

'Where are we actually going?'

'Where I always go when the most terrible things happen. Home.'

After a long windy walk, they came to an area that could at best, if you were being kind, be called shabby. A row of grim little terraced houses stretched out before them on either side of the cramped street. They all looked the same, weathered and bleak, apart from one whose tiny front garden was thronged with a rainbow of bright flowers and plants that climbed up and covered the whole front of the house in colour. Emily smiled to see them.

'No prizes for guessing which one's yours,' she said.

'Hrrm,' Tarkus muttered, as he tethered Painty amongst the flowers. As a keen student of his levels of awkward, Emily thought that Tarkus seemed even twitchier and more uncomfortable than normal.

'Y'know, I don't think I've ever actually asked you about your family before,' Emily said to break the silence. 'I'm a bad friend.'

'No, you're not.' He paused. 'Well, not deep down, anyway.'

'Not helping!' she said. 'I do remember you saying the thought of me and your mother ever meeting was terrifying.'

'Oh, it is,' he said with a terse scowl. 'Please, be on your best behaviour.'

'What do you mean? I always am.'

'Just don't do your . . . your mouth thing.'

'*What?!*' She glared at him, her eyes as flame-bright as his.

'That's exactly the tone it would be good to avoid. My mother can be . . . difficult.'

'The last person you told me was difficult turned out to be Cornelius, who was an enraged werewolf who nearly ate me.'

'Oh, she's nothing like that,' he said, as he opened the front door.

'Good.'

'She's much scarier.'

CHAPTER 7

A wave of heat and scent washed over Emily as she stepped into Tarkus's house. After the frigid chill of the streets, it was like a warm relaxing bath. The perfumed air filled her senses; it was intoxicating and wild. The scents made her nose twitch and fizz. One moment she could clearly smell sea salt and clear winds, next a bonfire of autumn, then a full florist's worth of flowers.

Her eyes were as overwhelmed as her nose. They had entered one long, low-beamed room, and everywhere and everything was hung and draped with wildly patterned fabrics, in every colour imaginable, and some unimaginable. It was a cross between a cottage and a Bedouin tent. After the moon-bleached colourless outside, it was a vivid assault on the eyes that, along with the warmth and fragrances, was enough to make her dizzy.

A woman sat on a low stool, illuminated by half a dozen candles, wrapped head to toe in a series of brightly patterned shawls. She leant forward intently over a piece of fabric stretched across a wooden frame, decorated with a rich pattern of leaves and flowers. A hand popped out of the shawls, holding a tiny delicate brush. She licked the bristles, then dipped the brush in a fleck of green paint on a palette balanced on her knee and daubed the tiniest bit on to one of the embroidered leaves.

'Mother?' said Tarkus. 'Sorry to interrupt, but—'

He was cut off by another hand that shot out of the shawls and was held up palm out in a clear 'Stop!' gesture. Tarkus stopped, and waited, as his mother turned back to the frame-held fabric and, twisting her fingers into an uncomfortable-looking shape, held them just over where she'd painted.

Emily did the eyebrows-raised, palms-upturned gesture that even here, 150 years ago, still meant 'What the heck?' Tarkus shook his head minutely, and stayed still. Normally, Emily would loudly make herself known in as rude a manner as the person ignoring her deserved, but she had promised Tarkus. She settled for an aggrieved sigh and bit her tongue, hanging on as time seemed to stretch out.

Suddenly, a clear tropical scent cut through the raucous mix of other smells. It was like a picture drawn for the nose. Emily could almost see the jungle that would smell like that – rich musky flowers, humid breezes, and thick mossy loam underfoot. She forgot all about her annoyance and lost herself in it.

With a single lithe movement, the shawl-wrapped woman slid off her stool and gracefully moved before them.

'Ah, the young woman from outside. Hecate's blessing on you as you enter our house.'

Her accent was a little thicker than Tarkus's. Her face was stern, and Emily could see where her son's perpetual frown had come from. She had the same fine brown skin as Tarkus and presumably the same pointy ears, although they were hidden under layers of fabric. Her yellow eyes throbbed with fire and spilt light on to her cheeks. She was pretty intimidating, Emily thought, for someone who probably wasn't more than five foot tall.

'Erm, thanks. Pleased to meet you, Mrs Poswa.'

Tarkus's mother didn't say anything else, but folded her arms and stared quite fixedly just above Emily's eyeline. Her nostrils flaring, she frowned and sniffed and stared some more. Emily felt terribly awkward. Her head started to itch and her hand started to rise up towards her hair.

'Erm, what is it?' Before she could help it, she'd patted

at her hair. 'Sorry if I'm a stinky mess, there's been quite a lot of hiding and trying not to die today.'

'Hmmm, it's strange,' said Tarkus's mum, taking one last big sniff of Emily and meeting her eye finally. 'Despite everything my son has said, you don't smell like "a reckless idiot with no sense of self-preservation or control of her tongue".'

Emily gawped and Tarkus groaned aloud.

'Mother!'

With that, Mrs Poswa's frown turned into a small but genuine smile, and she linked an arm through Emily's and walked her off towards the low seats by the fire. A cloud of something that smelt a lot like lilies spread around them.

'Let's get you in the warm, and you can tell me all about how your influence caused my terribly sensible son to become involved in an armed insurrection.'

'*Mother!*'

Emily was in the seat of honour by the fire and, after wriggling out of all her layers, was now at a very pleasant tropical beach temperature. Tarkus had fetched a thick aromatic drink that was part broth, part tea, served in a bowl with heaps of petals. Emily wasn't entirely sure about it, but she was downright delighted by the brightly coloured side dishes: seed cake and candied blossoms which tasted like sweets did in her dreams.

'Sorry to leave you standing there, dearest of hearts,' said Mrs Poswa, who had now formally introduced herself as 'a descendant of the great fallen khanate and thus a princess thrice removed, but you must call me Florqassum, dear'.

'Once charmed, that green pigment must be used or it sets. I've so little left now, I can't waste it.'

She shot a hard look at Tarkus and the flames licked out of her eyes. 'Particularly after somebody's ridiculous painted horse ate half of my remaining stocks.'

Tarkus flinched and ducked his head in shame.

'Don't worry, my mum's an artist too, so I'm used to weird— I mean, creative people.' Emily winced. Close one. 'What were you doing? It smelt incredible.'

Tarkus was already moving to fetch the frame without being asked. Emily didn't have any trouble at all believing that Florqassum had really been a princess at some point. Tarkus held the fabric up for Emily to see and as he did, the jungle scent wafted from it again, completely transporting Emily's senses.

She looked up at Florqassum with astonishment.

'I . . . it's . . . wow. It's like being there. That's amazing.'

Florqassum tapped her index fingers together and ducked her head in a bow. 'Ah, once I was an artist of some small repute. Since this MBDA nonsense about "Daylight sympathizers", well . . .' She waved the thought away with her hand. 'Now, I wash, dye and scent cloth instead, so that we need not starve.'

She gave a completely ingenuous smile as she looked at Tarkus.

'But it is safe in here, and so we must number our blessings.'

Tarkus sighed the sigh of a man who has been down this road before and knew it to be bumpy and thankless. 'Mother, please. You know there was no magic left outside. We could not have survived.' He looked down at his shoes. 'I know it's bad right now, but better this than the alternative.'

'Better, says the fallen princeling.' Florqassum's eyes flared as bright as the brazier. 'You, a master artist of the *charrat* who could conjure other worlds, reduced first to policing, now on the run!'

The air around her turned acrid, like burnt chillies. Tarkus closed his eyes for a moment, and when he opened them his face was calm.

'Mother, we've been over this. I like being a policeman, and I hope to be one again.' Sage gusted from him as he spoke. 'And for now, I will do what is necessary to put things right, and keep us all safe.'

His mother took a deep steadying breath and the chilli-taint changed to lemon balm.

'You are a good boy. We shall endure, as we always have.'

She reached over and patted his knee. 'For we blow with the wind and bring our scent to new lands, and they shall eventually find us sweet.'

'May they find us sweet.' She and Tarkus chanted the last part together and he gripped her hand as they did. Emily looked away from such an intimate family moment. As she did, she realized with a shock that she was being watched from a gap in between two cloths by a piercing set of orange-glowing eyes. She froze as, just below them, a bright green pair appeared too.

'Erm, Tarkus ... there's ...'

He followed her gaze and smiled.

'Ah, I was wondering when they'd make an appearance. They're very shy.'

He held out a hand and opened his mouth as if to speak but nothing came out but a complicated waft of scents. Emily's nose couldn't figure out what was going on, but two small, black-haired, giggling whirlwinds of colour ran across and hurled themselves on to Tarkus, knocking him back onto the cushions. The whirlwinds slowed down enough to become visible as two small girls, wrapped in shawls like Florqassum, but with their long black hair left loose. Their eyes glowed brightly, orange and green, as they grinned shyly at Emily from the safety of Tarkus's arms.

'My sisters, the two flowers. They're not of naming age yet, but this one's half-name is Naughty,' Tarkus said, squeezing the orange-eyed one, 'and this one's Noisy.' There were high-pitched squeals of outrage and they began to pull his beard off.

Florqassum shook her head indulgently at her heaving pile of children, and gestured Emily closer. 'Tell me, daughter of Daylight, can you stop this tide of hate? My little flowers cannot bloom in your world.'

'I . . .' Emily halted; she wasn't going to lie to those burning eyes. 'I don't know. It's all gone bad really quickly, but surely nobody would be stupid enough to turn the Great Working off?'

'People will do a great many terrible things if someone else can be blamed.' Florqassum's face was stern again. 'And now I hear them accusing your people of bringing the shadows that haunt us, and I worry as I haven't since our original exile here.'

She reached out to squeeze Emily's hand, and her grip was dry and as hot as a mug of tea.

'The rise of dark ideas does not come with threats of evil, you must understand, but with promises to restore pride and honour, to make you great again.'

She looked at Tarkus with his sisters squeezed close under each arm.

'So do what you can, daughter, but do not underestimate the stupidity and wilful blindness of scared people.'

She clapped her hands, and forced a smile on to her face.

'But enough of that. You must rest before revolution reclaims you. I will find more treats to put some weight on your undernourished bones.'

Emily's mind was so full that she could barely even think about the promised treats. Was the situation really that bad? This was getting very heavy and grown-up and she didn't know if she was up to it. She was distracted by a faint scratching noise from her bag. Was that . . . the sound of writing? She fumbled with the buckles and jammed her hand in excitedly to pull the card out, but squealed as something pointy went straight under her fingernail. She used some quite choice words, then opened the bag's flap wide this time, to find . . .

'Hog?' she said, in baffled amazement. 'How on earth?'

Half curled up into a ball on her emergency pants was the Hog, all brown prickles and black nose, and very soundly asleep. Just like he'd been in his hibernation hog-palace when she had *very definitely* left him at home. He hadn't been in there when she got her disguise out earlier either, had he? What the heck?

'What are you doing? Get the card out,' said Tarkus, looking over her shoulder. 'He's a very impressive hedge-hog, yes, but . . . ?'

'You don't understand, he wasn't, he's not . . .'

'He's clearly asleep, which is not unusual based on our acquaintance.' Tarkus looked exasperated. 'Now hurry up.

I heard the scratching too.'

He was right, there was more scratching and it wasn't the Hog.

She unearthed the Library card, gave the snoring Hog the mother of all suspicious looks, and closed the bag again.

The scratching was definitely coming from the card. The words she'd scrawled on it before were rippling and changing, the ink being shaped into thick Gothic capitals as if by the strokes of an invisible pen.

CLOCK

After a moment another word appeared underneath.

ASAP

'So,' said Tarkus. 'That obviously means . . .'

'Yup,' said Emily. 'Again. Man, I'm getting sick of those stairs.'

In the Midnight Hour there was only one clock that didn't need any other description – the Great Working, or Big Ben, if you were from the Daylight realm. The very heart of the magic spell that held the Hour out of time.

'Mother, we shall have to leave immediately, I'm sorry.'

'Oh, that's a pity, I was just about to unearth your baby daguerreotypes,' said Florqassum with a devilish wink at Emily.

'Really very immediately then,' said Tarkus. 'I shall have to leave Painty in your care for now.'

'If the accursed animal eats any more of my paint, I shall turn it into canvas,' said Florqassum, but didn't sound as if she really meant it.

Tarkus knelt to talk seriously to Naughty and Noisy. 'Now, you girls must draw Painty some grass with the green crayons I got you. It is a very important job.' They both nodded mutely, wide eyes burning with colour, as he gave them both a big squeeze. It made Emily think suddenly of the devil-baby. She hoped he was okay and that her mum wasn't too worried about her. Or angry. Who was she kidding...

Tarkus bowed quite formally to his mother, hand pressed to heart, and Emily realized 'ta-ra' probably wasn't going to cut it. She bowed her head, and tapped both her index fingers together as Florqassum had done earlier.

'Thank you for the welcome to your home, Princess. I find you sweet, and am honoured by your hospitality and hope I can return it someday.'

Florqassum's smile was nearly brighter than her eyes. She swooped and moved, her shawls flickering around her as she did a twirling bow of her own in response.

'You have brightened an old washerwoman's day. Get my rigid stick of a son to bring you again whenever you wish.'

She spoke over Emily's head to Tarkus.

'This one is *chashfrrk*. Guard her well.'

And then they were back outside in the cold and the stark moonlight of the street, and the colour and warmth faded like a dream.

Emily turned to look at Tarkus.

'What's a *chashfrrk*?'

'It means you smell a lot better than you look, I suppose.' He narrowed his eyes in thought. 'The direct translation is "looks like a dog dropping but smells like the rarest blossom".'

'Oh, great. I think.' She paused. 'So you're actually a prince then?'

'It's a very sensitive subject and one we are absolutely not discussing. Now or ever.' He looked particularly serious.

'Fair enough,' said Emily and was quiet for perhaps another two seconds. 'So have you got a crown? Or like a sceptre or something?'

Tarkus held his palm up into the moonlight, circled finger to thumb and stared at the heavens.

'Great Hecate, I beg you to give me the strength of mind to not push this vastly annoying child into a hedge.'

'Oh, charming. Prince Charming, in fact. Ha!'

The air around them took on a sulphurous tone as he glared at her, and it seemed a good time to change the subject.

'So, back to the clock then?' she said.

'It makes sense. The only reason I hadn't tried there already was because it's under heavy guard.' He frowned.

'Well, I've got my Library card, and you're in disguise. Can't we just walk in?'

'Not a chance. The MBDA have people all around it, "for our safety", apparently.' He narrowed his eyes. 'Plus we have no idea if the Library is there voluntarily or not. Why else would she have disappeared?'

'Man, I hadn't thought of that,' Emily gulped. 'Well, she said ASAP, so we better think of a way in.'

'Oh, I can think of one,' said Tarkus. 'I just really hate it.'

CHAPTER 8

'If this is going to take much longer, I'm going to have to start the meter again,' said the scar-browed, bolt-necked cabbie. Emily could hardly hear him over the whip of the wind. She clung on to the edge of the flying carpet as it flapped and trembled in the gusts.

'Whatever, mate. Just hold it still, can you?'

Kneeling on the carpet by her, green-cheeked and swaying, was Tarkus. He had the glowing Master Key in his hand, and was trying to guide it into a small keyhole in a pane of translucent white glass. The glass was part of a door, which was part of the lower clock face of one of the biggest clocks in the world. Above them, the vast black hands of the Great Working sat exactly at midnight, one atop the other, holding back time as they had since 1859.

The express carpet Tarkus had commandeered fluttered in the glowing emerald fog that wreathed the tower, and was all that separated them from a plunge down to the Houses of Parliament and Westminster and the very hard ground below. Emily tore her eyes away from the dizzying drop. She was okay with heights, but the tower made it all the more clear how terribly high they were. Tarkus was very much not okay with heights and appeared to be paralysed.

''Ere, you sure this is legit?' said the cabbie.

'Course it is. Routine inspection, ain't it? You've seen the badge and the card,' said Emily. 'Now keep it down and keep it steady. My colleague is just having a really good think about what he's going to inspect first.'

She inched closer. 'Tarkus,' she whispered. 'Are you okay? We really need to get in now or the guards are going to notice.'

'I am okay,' said Tarkus through gritted teeth. 'I simply cannot move.'

'Oh,' said Emily. His eyes were clamped shut and a sheen of sweat covered his face. The key flared in his hand, every bit as electric green as the vast arcs of sorcerous light that flickered through the fog.

'Look, let me help, okay? I'll do it very slowly.'

She reached out and wrapped his trembling hand in her

own. The static prickle of magic crawled through it from the key. His hand was warm under hers and she felt his trembling subside. He opened his eyes and looked at her.

'Ready?' she said, and he nodded with the tiniest of movements. They leant out together over the dizzying drop and the key warped under their hands, matching the size of the brass keyhole. It twisted, clicked, and the glass door came open.

'There you go,' she crowed. 'Easy-peasy lemon-squeezy, and Big Ben's your uncle.'

'Actually,' the cabbie tutted, 'I think you'll find it's only the bell that is called Big Ben, the tower is actually called—'

'Oh, shut up, Frankenstein!' they both said together.

With the rigid limbs of total terror, Tarkus clambered on to the slim ledge and fell gratefully if not gracefully through the doorway. Emily followed him. Behind them came an aggrieved voice.

'It's the bloomin' doctor who's called Franken— Oh, why do I bother!'

Emily pulled the door shut and cut off both him and the wind. She turned and found Tarkus kneeling, both hands flat out and his head pressed to the floor.

'Are . . . are you praying?'

'No, I am simply staying as close to the ground as I can.'

She kicked him in the bum.

'Come on, doofus.'

They were in the huge bell mechanism room at the very top of the clock tower. The room was a vast cube, and its four towering walls were the white glass panes of the clock faces. Moonlight and the eerie green glow of sorcery shone through the translucent glass, throwing twisted shadows from the metalwork. Great rods joined the clock faces to the clockwork engine and the pendulum on the level below their feet. Above them the great bells hung like vast metal bats in the belfry. In the middle of the four quarter bells hung the heavyweight champion of the bell world, Big Ben itself. An iron whale of a thing, frozen in the very moment of ringing out midnight by the spell that cradled the world.

'Whoa!' shouted Emily, clutching at her chest as one of the lightning surges revealed a figure floating in the shadows ahead of them. A woman, extremely tall and thin, long black hair cascading down over a white lace gown. Her face was bleak and drawn, her gaze empty, even as her eyes flickered with the black ink of all the words that filled her. It was the Library: Older Power, one of the Sisters Three, the personification of Language, and technically Emily's boss.

'Damn it, Booky, you nearly gave me a heart attack.'

The Library said nothing, just stared past them.

'Where have you been?' demanded Tarkus, and looked immediately shocked at himself.

There was a long pause as the Library blinked slowly and seemed to see them for the first time.

'Here,' she said eventually, then nodded. 'We have been here.'

'Lady, Great Lady,' said Tarkus, who had reverted to his usual policy of being very formal around demigods. 'I have sought you for some time now, to deliver grave tidings.' Emily thought the way he dropped into posh court speech was quite cute. The whole prince thing made more sense now.

'The vile Make Britain Dark Again party are using the time shadows to their advantage. They seek to rally Parliament and the people to turn off this Great Working and leave the Hour.'

The Library wafted a hand, as if brushing the MBDA away.

'They are unimportant.'

'What?! They could ruin us all. My family!' said Tarkus, his eyes flashing fire. 'I insist you stop them!'

'I hold infinity in the palm of my hand, and eternity in an hour,' said the Library, finally focusing on Tarkus, her eyes flooding with ink. 'Be assured, to break this greatest of spells, they would need to pass me.' It wasn't just her eyes that were changing; she was suddenly even taller, and shadows of ink raced over her white gown, her hair spread out around her as if she floated deep underwater. 'And I am not to be tested.'

Tarkus bowed his head, but he didn't look convinced.

'Then why are you here?' said Emily, who wasn't that

convinced either. The pause was even longer this time. Emily was wondering whether she could tactfully get a snack out of her bag when . . .

'Because of things that have not happened yet.' The Library was looking out into the sky of London, where the hulking forms of the time shadows loomed over the old city.

'Because something is coming. Because I feel a great—'

'Disturbance in the Force?' said Emily's mouth before her brain could stop it. The Library's inky eyes narrowed. Emily shut up.

'A great unease,' the Library continued. 'What I feel is the future, and it is bright.'

'Well, that sounds good!'

'Bright like fire, and torches, and the blade of sunlight cutting our people to pieces.' Her eyes teemed with blackness and she stared off into a world only she could see.

'Really less good.'

'You claim to see the future?' said Tarkus, even more greenly pale than before.

'No, the future can see us.' The Library traced a finger along the metalwork of the clock parts. 'The Great Working exists outside time, but somehow the future is leaking in.'

'My lady, I have finished my analysis.' The deep growly voice came from the stairwell and made Emily jump again. People really needed to stop doing that – she was twitchy enough as it was. From the stairs came a large figure, bulky with muscle. The hefty shape was draped in tweed, with an oil-spattered leather apron cinched around its front. The thick furry legs that projected from beneath were jointed in reverse, like a dog's, and ended in giant clawed paws. It stepped into a beam of light, revealing a ferocious mask of fur and bared teeth.

'Cornelius!' Emily squealed with delight, making the hulking werewolf wince and clap a hand to his sensitive ears. A sharp-toothed grin emerged though, as she shot over to give him a hug. Professor Cornelius Snark was one of the original magical engineers of the clock. Emily had once nearly enraged him into eating her, but they'd ended up rather liking one another.

'Ah, young Miss Emily.' He gave her a narrow-eyed look. 'Of course you'd be here.'

'What's that supposed to mean?' she said.

'These are troubled times, and it has been my observation –' his furry brow wrinkled – 'that you do not so much borrow trouble, as grab it then refuse to give it back.'

She didn't have to look to know that Tarkus was nodding behind her.

'Oi, don't you start too,' she said. 'What's going on, Cornelius?'

'As I was about to report to m'lady here, I am at a loss.'

He produced a handkerchief from his waistcoat pocket and began to wipe oil off his fingers as he spoke. 'You have to understand that this clockwork isn't simply frozen in time, it is in fact straining against all of reality to remain that way.'

He proceeded to use his now oil-covered hanky to clean his monocle. 'It is a fish swimming so hard against the current that it seems to stand still while the river flows on around it.'

Emily squinted. She had forgotten quite how aquatic Cornelius's explanations could be.

'And it is still swimming. The Great Working is functioning perfectly.' He put his oily monocle back in, then frowned in confusion at his sudden blindness. 'I cannot account for these shadowy apparitions. It makes no sense.'

'The future is ahead of us,' said the Library. Which was where, Emily thought, the future was supposed to be, but it sounded much more threatening when the Library said it.

'Well, all these shadows, I recognize them,' said Emily, trying to puzzle it out. 'They *are* your future, but they're things from my present.'

Cornelius's ears pricked up as he listened. 'Well, technically we exist outside of time, so "future" is an outdated – ha! – concept.'

She silenced him by reaching up to put a finger on the end of his muzzle.

'Hush puppy. Let's keep it super simple,' she said, squinting as her brain corkscrewed sideways trying to work it through. 'If all the shadows come from my present, then isn't the cause going to be in the present too?'

Cornelius gasped and his monocle popped out. 'Wait there. Nobody speak.' He held a furry paw up. 'I must concentrate on magical algebra.'

With that, he closed his eyes and began muttering. They all shuffled awkwardly as the wolf growled to himself. Even the Library didn't seem to know where to look.

'Ha!' barked Cornelius suddenly, making Emily squeal and jump in the air. He looked quizzically at her and continued.

'It all makes sense now! There must be an outside influence or,' he paused and scrunched his snout up in thought, 'or possibly an inside outfluence.'

'Outside where? Here?' Emily turned to look at the glass walls.

Cornelius harrumphed and waved his paws wide, indicating vast magical distances. 'No, *outside* outside. Your world. The—'

'Daylight!' Emily finished for him. 'But that must mean . . .' She caught Tarkus's bleak expression as she spoke what they were both thinking. 'Who do we know who totes wants the Hour to go boom and was last seen escaping into the Daylight realm?'

'The Nocturne,' Tarkus said through gritted teeth.

'Such sweet compulsion doth in Music lie,' said the

Library. 'I have feared for some time that my sister was behind this. Come with me.'

And with that she turned and marched towards the stairs, leaving Emily and Tarkus to scurry in her wake.

The Pendulum Room was an imposing sight. The huge clock engine was like an upended steam train, wheels and cogs and clockwork and all. What wasn't normally here, though, was the tall thin woman lying horizontally in mid-air over it, hands crossed over her chest, and surrounded by a moving gauzy haze of colour. It was Art, the Library's other, non-evil, sister, and Emily's friend. Her eyes were closed, her face was pale and the thin tracery of silver scars that laced it stood out like shining lines. Emily had once seen a famous painting of a drowned girl, still beautiful, but lying just under the surface of the water. Art looked just like that, but her river was colour and it flowed over and round her while she lay as if dead. Emily stepped up and seized the Library's sleeve.

'Tell me right now that she's okay.'

'She is as well as she can be.' The Library nodded slowly. 'As its original architect, she holds the Great Working together against these shadows.'

The Library looked enormously tired, and oddly human. 'I feed her what power I can, and keep her safe.'

'We must talk of your other sister, Great Lady,' said Tarkus, his face set with grim determination. 'What are we to do about the Nocturne?'

The Nocturne. *Man.* Emily's whole brain flooded with memories of her, none of them good. Older Power, arch-enemy, primal personification of music gone really bad, like death-metal-jazz-fusion bad. Also quite keen to blow up the Midnight Hour so she could pinch all its magic.

'Your path is clear,' said the Library.

'It is?' said Emily.

'You must find her outside, in the Daylight world, and discover how she is causing the time shadows.'

'Oh sure, no bother. How hard can it be?' said Emily. Tarkus nodded along with her. She turned to him, eyes wide. 'Sarcasm!'

She whirled back to the Library.

'How am I supposed to do that? I'm not even faintly magic outside, and barbed wit isn't going to get us too far.' She had a nasty thought. 'In fact, how is she even using powers out there? There's no magic. How is she even alive, in fact?'

'Magic poured out with her when she escaped from the Hour,' said the Library. 'How she has kept it, I do not know, but she may be very dangerous.'

'Oh, it gets better!'

'You are only to investigate, then report back. Do not be

seen,' the Library said. 'I will meet you at Paternoster Row, the usual shop, next midnight.'

'I feel like you're not listening somehow,' said Emily.

'You are our only operative who has a chance – no one knows the Daylight like you do.'

'Do not fear, I will not leave your side,' said Tarkus.

Emily looked at him, with his flaming yellow eyes and pointed ears.

'*How* is this my life?'

The Library spoke quietly then, most unlike her usual sonorous tones.

'She . . . was not always so.'

'Great Lady?'

'My sister was not always the Nocturne. Not what she is now. She was once the Madrigal and she was kind.' The Library reached out to take Art's hand where she lay. 'When the Black Death nearly swept your world clean, the music stopped and she was extinguished.'

She spoke without looking at them.

'When she came back she was . . . different.'

Emily managed, by a great effort of will, to not say anything offensive at this point.

'But once she was kind. I would just wish you to know that.'

They left her there then, holding her other sister's hand, black tears seeping down her cheeks.

CHAPTER 9

At midnight precisely, Emily and Tarkus unlocked an old door at the top of the Great Working and crossed between worlds, back into the Daylight realm. The tower was so old that little changed, apart from the dim fluorescent lights now glinting in the stairwell.

'Well,' said Emily, then almost wet herself in fright as a vast sound filled the whole world. The great bell ringing out midnight above them. After eleven more colossal chimes, the silence afterward was filled by the ringing in her ears. 'Obviously, I was expecting that.' She rose up from her huddled crouch, unpicking her terribly tight jeans from a self-inflicted wedgie. 'Erm, Flowers, hello?'

Tarkus was standing stock-still with an expression of almost delirious delight on his face.

'Tarkus, did the bells damage your brain?'

He grinned at her. 'I've never actually heard it before. Only on my little night watch. It's wonderful.' He cocked his head at her curiously. 'What?'

'It's . . . it's your eyes, they've gone out.'

He blinked and frowned. His constantly smouldering eyes were dark. She could see for the first time that they were an off-topaz colour, with triangular irises, but their flame was extinguished.

'It is how we are without magic.'

He sniffed experimentally, then again, then harder, like he had a really bad cold and no tissues. Then he held his hand out and his eyes narrowed in concentration, and his brow furrowed and . . . nothing happened. He dropped his hand and sagged back against the wall. 'Nothing. I can't smell anything, and I can't *charrat*.'

'Eh?'

'I cannot feel or manipulate or create scent.'

'But you're okay?'

'Ha!' His eyes, fiery or not, burnt into her. 'I am, as you say, okay. As okay as you'd be if you lost your sight unexpectedly, or a hand perhaps.'

'Oh man, dude, I'm sorry. I didn't mean . . .'

'It is fine. I knew what going through meant.' Tarkus

sighed. 'We have a while before the other effects start, so let's get moving.'

'Hang on, what other effects?'

'Oh, the usual – sickness, organ failure, death and so on.'

'WHAT?!' Emily grabbed his arm. 'What do you mean? I'm magic too, and I'm okay out here. I just can't do Pooka stuff.'

'The folk of the night differ. We, the ghûl, are more magic reliant.' He smiled gently, his gaze, his new gaze, on hers. 'That is why the Midnight Hour is so important to my family. Because they will die slowly without magic.'

They stood looking at each other in charged silence.

'Then why did you come, you massive eejit?' she said, softly.

'Because I would not leave you alone to face our enemy, nor my family without a champion.'

Tarkus produced a nightshade brolly from his apparently bottomless coat pockets, and poked her in the arm with it.

'And because you are a significant threat to public order who shouldn't be let out on her own. Now, come along, we have work to do.'

After a knee-bruising walk down the endless staircase, a surprisingly neatly managed escape from a national monument was effected using the nightshade and Tarkus's Master Key. They now stood near Westminster Bridge, with the clock towering above them, and Tarkus had, it seemed to Emily, gone full tourist on her.

He looked up, froze, then, leaning on his closed nightshade, he started to spin around very slowly, eyes wide and mouth open. 'And they say there is no magic here,' he whispered.

She did a little spin herself. The bridge in front, gleaming under the orange of the street lights, the vast white Ferris wheel of the London Eye towering above it on the other bank, the glistening constellation of buildings down the long arc of the Thames. Time shadows no more, now they were a mountain range of glass and steel glowing in the night.

'Lights,' he said, 'so many lights. However do they do it?'

He turned back to what was the brightest light in his own London, the Great Working. Here the clock tower didn't gleam with the emerald sheen of magic but was picked out by an array of spotlights, still leaving it bright against the night sky.

'But where,' he said, his voice alarmed, 'is the moon?'

'Erm, it's not always there, you know.'

'Ha! I'd forgotten. So strange for it not to be in the sky.' He laughed. 'I feel foolish.'

'I'll never mention it again,' she said, filing it away under things she would definitely mention again.

'Erm, is that a normal thing here?' he said, still looking up.

'What?' she said indulgently. He'd probably seen a plane and was worried about it being an iron bird or something, poor old Victorian that he was.

'That person running down the clock tower towards us.'

'What?!'

Above them, hotfooting it down the completely sheer side of the tower, was a black-clad figure who shimmered slightly, as if dressed in glass. It made Emily giddy to watch. How could anyone possibly . . . The figure grew closer, black outfit glinting, a flash of deep red streaming out behind it at the top. That was worryingly familiar . . . but a more immediate concern was how would they stop? Were they just going to run straight into the ground? The impossible runner was sprinting now, pumping arms and lifting knees and, at about thirty feet off the ground, they launched themselves off the building and into the air. Gracefully tucking into a tight somersault, they cleared all the railings then landed lightly on their feet not far from Emily and Tarkus. The impact took the figure down into a deep crouch, and forced a wave of long lustrous red hair forward to cover their face.

'Whoa, superhero landing,' said Emily under her breath. 'So cool.'

As the figure bounced back to their feet and flicked their hair back (such great hair), Emily was already regretting her words. It was Bron. Blooming Bron. Rogue Pooka, Nocturne's assistant, queen of the dramatic entrance, possessor of great hair, and really big Emily hater. Also, regrettably, cousin.

'Ye!' Never had one word sounded so like an accusation. Bron's beautiful face was twisted into an ugly snarl. 'I knew I smelt ye. And yer pet eejit.'

'Before we get on to the inevitable argy-bargy, I've got to know, how did you do that?' said Emily.

Bron never could handle Emily's habit of saying something random. She could also never resist the urge to show off.

'Oh, wouldn't you like to know,' she said, and ran two thumbs down the lapels of the really rather swish black trouser suit she was wearing. She normally wore gothic leather and lace, so this was an unexpectedly snazzy departure. It was black but glittered with ... were those stars? The distant radiance of the cosmos moved within the fabric; it was as if she were wearing a slice of the night sky.

'So, it's the suit. Gotcha,' said Emily.

Bron sneered. 'My lady armours me with magic beyond what you can imagine. I am her sword.'

'Funny, because I've always thought of you as more of a bog brush.'

'Your "lady" is a criminal who threatens our very existence,' Tarkus cut through the bickering in loud harsh tones. 'Why were you on the clock tower? What part do you play in her vile plans?'

Bron smiled her oh-so-superior smile. 'I pave the way for her glory.'

'Glory?' said Tarkus in strangled tones. '*Glory?*' His previous look of wonder was long gone, now replaced with a mask of quiet fury. 'You leave me no choice but to arrest you, and take you in for further questioning.'

'Erm, Tarkus, you're not even a police—' started Emily, but it was too late. Bron had never been one to shy away from a fight.

'You dare!' She hissed and her Midnight suit rippled with starlight. 'I'm going to make you so unlucky you'll explode.'

Even as she spoke, Tarkus popped the nightshade open, like someone else might have cocked a pistol.

'Now you're not the only person with magic.' His eyes lit back up like torches, as bright as Emily had ever seen them. He grinned, but it was all teeth and no humour. An acidic scent filled the air around him, and made Bron blink and rub at her eyes. Righteously angry Tarkus was kinda scary. The riverside was quiet at this time of night, but the occasional passers-by were starting to stare.

'Whoa there!' Emily stepped in between them. 'Bron, I

know we can't stand each other, but surely you care about your family?'

'What do you know about family, half-breed?' Bron snarled.

'Nice. Look, did you know the Pooka are being blamed for the time shadows?' said Emily. 'Did you know there's great big horrid killer-hand things hunting them down because of it?'

Bron's brow furrowed. 'That's not true.'

'If I say it more slowly, will it help? The Pooka are being hunted.' Emily watched Bron carefully as she spoke. 'The clan are being punished for whatever it is you're doing out here.'

Bron was angling her head uncomfortably from side to side now, as if not quite able to hear clearly.

'And that's what you were doing up there, right? Something to affect the spell. For *her*.' As Emily spoke the last word, Bron visibly twitched. For a professional criminal she had a bad poker face.

'And it's just what she wants, because I crossed her.' Emily had the sudden clarity that you can sometimes get from saying something aloud. 'I crossed her and so she's hurting my family. *Our* family.'

Bron actually took a step back. 'But my lady wouldn't do that! The Pooka are to be mine to lead in the new world. She never lies.'

'No, but she's pretty good at only telling part of the truth. Did she happen to say how many Pooka would be left in this new world?'

Bron's proud face was tight and creased now. Her fingers worried at a silver chain around her neck, and Emily had a tantalizing glimpse of a tarnished silver coin dangling from it. A coin twin to the ones she wore around her own neck – a bad penny.

'Bron, things are really bad in there. What is she making you do to the clock?'

'It . . . it needs to be bad so it can get better. Bad so it can get better.' Bron repeated it like a mantra, her worry-riven face smoothing as she did. 'So people know to make the change.'

Emily knuckled her temple. 'Is that what you think or what you've been told? Is she still in your head? Even out here?'

The Nocturne's music could make people do things. Pooka were mainly immune, but not if they listened willingly, and Bron had.

'I think that yer lies don't matter now, sure,' said Bron, with some steel in her voice again. 'The last adjustment has already been made, there's nothing can stop what's to come.'

Her eyes were shining with a manic light. Was there a hint of distant music in the air? Suddenly, with a hiss like a

⟨footer⟩

leaky bouncy castle, Bron was gone and a great black hound with red eyes jumped snarling from where she'd been standing. It cannoned between Emily and Tarkus, knocking them both sprawling, and was off across the road and down the riverside pavement at full speed.

'I thought that went well, don't you?' Emily said to Tarkus as they staggered back to their feet. 'Despite the whole totally getting seen by the enemy bit.'

She looked for Bron, but she'd already vanished from sight, leaving stunned late-night walkers in her wake. 'Man, she's got proper magic if she can change out here.'

Tarkus ignored her, and stared at the clock tower.

'They're doing something to the clock out here, to affect the spell in the Hour,' he said, jaw tight. 'We need to get back up and try to fix it, then warn the Library and—'

'Know a lot about fixing giant magic clocks, do you?' said Emily, then held her hand up as he started to reply. 'Rhetorical! Look, we can't tell the Library anything until next midnight, and we've just been handed a golden opportunity.'

She pointed after Bron. 'Where's the first place Professor McBronagle is going to run to now she's seen us?'

'Her foul mistress,' Tarkus nodded, a grim smile on his lips.

'Exactamundo. And if you'll share the nightshade, I reckon I can track her down with the old Pooka nose!'

It wasn't as easy as she'd hoped. Nothing ever was, she was starting to realize. With the nightshade open above them, spreading its little bit of Midnight Hour magic, her Pooka senses came alive, but filled immediately with the reek of the city. The traffic fumes alone were almost too much, and combined with the smells generated by the sheer bulk of humanity modern London contained, it was over-whelming. She'd managed it though, had calmed herself and focused her Pooka abilities. Using the hound's nose, she had found the foreign tang of magic on the air, of Pooka power, of bad-luck metal, and the rippling star-dark magic of the suit.

And so they followed it, as the trail weaved through the city. It was quieter now than the madness of the daytime but still busy. Soho roared with noise and people spilt out of late-night bars on to pavements. The filthy reek of tobacco made her hypersensitive magic nose sting and she nearly gagged. They attracted the odd strange look, but London had seen stranger things than a girl in a cape with a curious umbrella and a young man wearing too much leather. Particularly in Soho.

They paused on the edge of Chinatown to buy Tarkus a beanie from an all-night shop. It was covered in kawaii creatures with big eyes that blinked cutely, but at least it covered his ears. Bron's scent kept heading north, and Emily was grateful for her cousin's reliance on magic. If she'd just had the sense to get on a night bus, they'd have been stuffed. The trail weaved west to travel inside the edge of Regent's Park, as if Bron was as sick of the smells of London's streets as Emily was.

After that moment of quiet green peace, the trail led them into the dirtier streets of the pulsing heart of Camden Town, still throbbing with the sounds of music pounding from behind brick walls. And there it stopped dead. The hound scent faded out, the silver tarnish of the coin gave up, even the strange tang of the suit disappeared. It was as if Bron had walked into outer space and vanished.

By the time they'd admitted defeat, having circled the block repeatedly to no avail, it was so late, it was early. Even all the pubs and clubs had turned off the lights and gone silent. They had lost the trail, their only clue to find the Nocturne, and they were all alone on the streets of London with nowhere to go. What were they supposed to do now?

CHAPTER 10

Seven hours later, Emily and Tarkus staggered out of the all-night screening of *The Lord of the Rings* that she'd found for them to sleep in. They were both stiff and creaking, and coming out into daylight was a shock. Even more so for Tarkus. He winced, and scrabbled for his smoked-glass lenses.

'You okay, Legolas?'

'Yes, I had simply forgotten about the sun,' he said. 'That's two major celestial bodies now. I trust you're keeping count?'

'You know it.'

It was far from the most beautiful part of London, but

the sky was blue and there were even a few birds singing. Tarkus swayed, and she saw a tear run out from under his glasses.

'Tee? You sure you're okay? I know you were upset when Sam didn't marry Frodo at the end, but it's only a film.'

'No, no, it's not that injustice, it's . . .' He trailed off, his voice thick with emotion. 'Could we go somewhere there are trees? I'd just like to see . . .'

'Sure,' she said. 'Sure, come on.' And she reached out to take his hand, surprising them both. She led him through the already quickening streets of harried people with bags and coffees, all staring down at their phones and never looking up. She took him down to the canal where they stepped under the sheltering fronds of a willow tree. Emily let go of Tarkus's hand so he could press it to the bark instead. He took off his glasses to look up into leaves lit emerald and jade by the sun, and the tears ran freely down his cheeks.

They didn't speak for a little while, then he sniffed a particularly violent sniff, and wiped his eyes on his sleeve.

'Thank you.'

'S'okay. Want to talk about it?'

'I . . . Perhaps.' His eyes were red, and his curious, triangular topaz pupils were blurry still. 'Not all Night Folk existed purely in the night, you know. Just as you don't only live in the day.'

He gestured at the thin sun through the branches. 'We

ghûl used to live in both because of the plants. We gave up a great deal for our refuge in the Midnight Hour, not least the sun.'

He turned to her and joined his index fingers to thumbs in the ghûl expression of ritual thanks.

'It is a privilege to experience this, I thank you.' His tranquil expression changed to something darker. 'And yet I pray I never see this again, because it will mean we failed.'

The pregnant moment was broken by Emily's stomach rumbling.

'Right, if we have to track down my arch-nemesis, then I'm totally going to need breakfast first,' she said. 'Let me introduce you to a magical creation of the Daylight world known as the Pop Tart.'

Several thousand calories later they walked under Camden Lock's iconic bridge. Tarkus had rejected the Pop Tarts as 'containing nothing of nature or goodness whatsoever', but had proved to be pretty down for the green smoothie. He slurped as he walked.

'Right, this can't be that complicated,' said Emily, restored by the huge sugar rush. 'The Nocturne is here somewhere, I just know it.'

'That is purely speculation,' said Tarkus, frowning. 'Not deduction. We need to approach this logically.'

'This is logic! Bron came here and just . . . disappeared.' She glared around, eyes narrowed. 'That doesn't mean we lost her, that means she got where she was going and got picked up or hidden or something.'

She nodded firmly, convincing herself.

'It's a clue— Oof!'

She had walked straight into Tarkus, who had stopped in the middle of the pavement to gawp at the brightly coloured mayhem of giant elephants, dragons, scorpions and dark angels that erupted out of the frontages of the shops on either side of the road.

'Tarkus!' she hissed. 'Stop being such a tourist.'

'Sorry, it is . . . the same, but so different,' he said, still gazing around.

'This is exactly how I feel in the Hour when we go somewhere like Knightsbridge, then end up having to deal with some dudes in armour or something.' She sighed. 'It's just different here. Things have changed.'

'They certainly have,' he said, shaking his head. 'Back home this is all dragon stables, piano factories and music halls.'

'Music halls . . . you know what, that could be it.' Emily bit her lip in sudden thought. 'The last time I found her, she was in the opera house.'

'I follow your reasoning.' Tarkus nodded as she spoke. 'She is drawn to music and musical places. Is there still such a thing round here?'

'Camden kinda *is* music,' Emily grinned. 'So Bron coming here makes sense now.' She frowned then. 'But everything's closed in the daytime. Hmmm.'

A group of cackling girls walked past in a rainbow of colour. There was a great deal of leather, spandex and eyeliner, along with hair colours that were even brighter than the shopfronts.

'Ha! Got it. There's somewhere else that blares music all day long. Follow those cyber-goths!'

Even mid-morning, Camden Market was packed with people, all drawn in like magpies to the incredible Technicolor treasure house of stuff that waited within. Latex clothes in lurid colours, band T-shirts beyond number, fabulously studded platform footwear, wildly patterned rugs, fragrant joss sticks, and amidst it all the constant thumping of music – hundreds of different bands from hundreds of different speakers.

'So much . . . of everything!' Tarkus was wide-eyed. 'How are we to find her in this bewilderment?'

'You see bewilderment, I see Camden,' Emily grinned. Emily was a Camden veteran. She had been before many times with her mum, who loved it here. The thought of her mum was like a sudden stab to the heart. Being on an adventure in the Hour was one thing, but she was back in her London now, Daylight London, and she . . . totally couldn't think about this now. She promised herself she would the moment she'd figured out where the Nocturne was. There was a bit of her that said this was a really bad plan but she ignored it for now.

They did a circuit of the market, threading their way through the stalls and down all the little alleys, then they did it again because they found nothing, apart from a few excellent bargains that Emily made a note of for later. The place was all full of weirdness, but not a supervillain in sight.

Even through her frustration, Emily couldn't help but notice that Tarkus had gone green and sweaty.

'Tee, I keep saying this, but are you okay?'

'I am struggling somewhat, I confess. The lack of magic is taking its toll.'

'Well, let's go and sit out the way and put the nightshade up for a minute, yeah?'

She led him to Horse Tunnel Market, knowing it was quieter there. She found them a seat on a low wall by the entrance and they sat underneath the amazing horse sculptures – a multitude of metal stallions bursting out of the wall and rearing up. Tarkus erected the nightshade and leant back into its magic-laden gloom with a sigh of relief.

'Dude!' said Emily. 'Put your shades on, or you'll end up in a lab.'

He fumbled his smoked-glass lenses over his flaming eyes, and sat there in his leather coat, basking in the midnight glow of the nightshade. As it was Camden, he didn't look even slightly out of place.

Tarkus suddenly sat up straighter.

'Can you hear that?'

'What?'

He moved his head around, listening to something she couldn't hear, then gestured her closer. As she sat with him under the nightshade she could hear a thin haunting melody, like a harp singing out over a frozen lake. She moved out of the nightshade's range and the music stopped immediately.

'It's magic music!'

Tarkus was on his feet in an instant and she followed him. The melody grew louder as they turned on to Saddle Row, a narrow pathway lined with vibrant shops. Each shopfront was an ornate wooden archway set into the brickwork, leading to a deep tunnel of vintage wares. The music lamented and moaned and grew ever louder as they made their way down the path. They must be close.

Tarkus stopped dead in front of an archway. It was topped with a carved horse's head and the tunnel beyond was empty all the way to the back, filled only with the deepest shadow. The music became louder and louder, resonating and growing into the most beautiful sound

Emily had ever heard, and then it was gone.

Suddenly the archway wasn't empty anymore. At the back of the deep tunnel, the shadows shifted and merged and became a vast black sphere, completely filling the tall arch. It was full of silken blackness and the gleam of stars, as if the night sky had been scooped up and brought to earth. This miniature cosmos shifted and the Nocturne floated into view at the centre of the sphere.

The Nocturne: Older Power, arch-nemesis and president of the Bad Things Should Happen to Emily Society. Diaphanous blue silks floated around her in the cosmic darkness, and her black hair drifted out like a galaxy all of its own. She had been damaged and weak when Emily last saw her but now she glowed from within. Her skin shone alabaster and her sapphire eyes flashed like the sun breaking through the deepest waters of the ocean.

Emily suddenly had the awful realization that they had been so focused on finding her that they hadn't got a single plan for what to do when they did.

A gentle smile played over the immortal's lips.

'I believe you wished to see me?' Her voice was melodic as ever, honeyed tones that filled the ears with gold. Her expression was as welcoming as if she'd just invited them to a tea party.

'Errm, yeah, right, totally,' Emily said coolly. 'You, your, erm—'

'Madam,' interrupted Tarkus, stepping into the gloomy tunnel. 'We come to order you to cease and desist from your heinous actions against the Midnight Hour. Otherwise we will be forced to take measures against you.'

'And what actions would these be?' she said, her eyebrow arching in benign curiosity. 'I am but a poor exile, will you not tell me of the charges against me?'

Now it was Tarkus's turn to stumble. 'Your, ah, obvious attempts to, erm, undermine the stability of the Hour, and . . .'

The eyebrow arched higher. 'Is this something you have proof of?'

'Errrm . . .'

'Oh give it a break! We all know it's you,' said Emily, who found anger had restored her ability to talk quite handily, thank you. 'Blooming Bron told us so. Stop the time shadow nonsense or we'll . . .'

She ran out of words as quickly as she'd started.

'Or you'll what, exactly?' said the Nocturne, staring at her like a snake does a mouse. 'You don't have anything, do you?'

Her awful laughter bubbled up and made Emily wince like nails being dragged down a blackboard.

'I allowed you to find me because, I will admit, you've proven annoyingly resourceful before.' The Nocturne swayed in her private sphere of night. 'But now I can see you have nothing. No hidden cards. No idea of the game that's being played, even.' Her wide shark smile was now definitely less tea party, more torture chamber, and her eyes glowed with power. *Power . . . hmmm, hang on.*

'Nothing to say, child, hmmm?' She smiled at Emily, colder than a glacier.

'Only this. You hate me, and him. Me more though, obvs,' Emily said, and the Nocturne inclined her head. It was true, she really did.

'And you've got magic here somehow, so, like, why aren't we dying a horrible musical death or something?'

The Nocturne's face went blank.

'You . . . you're stuck inside there, aren't you?' said Emily.

The Nocturne still said nothing, only glared. Tarkus looked at Emily in astonishment, a smile slowly spreading across his face.

'It's a magical hamster ball,' Emily said, then, seeing how the Nocturne bobbed on the eddies of magic within her globe, 'No, it's a fishbowl.'

She did a little happy dance, a soft shoe shuffle of joy as she spoke.

'You're trapped. You've stolen magic from the Hour but it only works in your bowl, right?' she said, her smile widening. 'That's why Bron's running around for you. You're . . . you're a goldfish!'

The hiss from the Nocturne was like a striking snake,

and with a snake's speed she was pressed up against the wall of the black pearlescent globe, clawing at Emily, who hurled herself back and stumbled on to her bum. Emily looked up to find the Nocturne had completely vanished, but then . . .

'You! You and your mouth! You can do nothing but taunt me,' snarled the Nocturne's unmistakeable voice. Emily had fallen out from under the nightshade. The sphere and its prisoner were invisible without magic. The perfect hiding place.

'The great forces I have unleashed are now unstoppable. I need but bide my time,' said the Nocturne, and Emily could hear the smile in her voice. 'I've already won.'

'You said that last time, as I remember,' said Tarkus as he helped Emily up and under the brolly. 'How did that turn out? You fleeing in tatters, now forced to live in a cage.'

He took his glasses off and stared her down, his eyes roaring flames. 'The same will happen again.'

'Let me tell your fortune, ghûl. There is nothing you can do,' said the Nocturne, sneering, and distant screeching strings underlined her words. 'The clock will start, the spell will shatter, your family will die, and all because people are *weak*.'

'That's not going to happen!' shouted Tarkus, shaking with fury. Emily had never seen him so angry. His eyes were at risk of setting fire to his beanie. The music flared up louder around them, angry and insistent this time. He stepped closer. 'You will not harm my family.'

The Nocturne was watching Tarkus like a dog does an unfinished plate on the table. Furious, his arms gesturing wildly, he came dangerously close to the black globe. The Nocturne grabbed for him and Emily just managed to yank him back by his coat. They both ended up on the floor again, gasping, as the Nocturne grinned down at them.

'It is not just the present day that I can send, but any happening in London since the Great Working began. History is mine to wield as a weapon.'

Her gaze was locked on Emily's as if they were the only two people in the world.

'Before I sent shadows, now I send fire.' It was conversational, friendly even. A simple declaration of the terrible things she was going to do. 'The Midnight Hour is already finished, it just doesn't know it yet.'

'The Library will stop you!' Emily shouted.

'My sisters will meet their end even before the Hour does.' The Nocturne laughed, a sound like icy rain and bad dreams.

Emily's throat was very dry all of a sudden. All she could do was shake her head.

The Nocturne delicately trailed a finger along the curve of the globe as she spoke. 'Then I will destroy each and every thing that you love, before I take your life.' She gave them one final glance, her eyes flashing cobalt, then dismissed them as beneath notice.

'Go now, you bore me, and I have constellations to move to my whim.'

The globe faded to pure midnight then vanished, leaving only one diamond-pure note of exquisite agony behind it.

CHAPTER 11

They staggered blindly away from the market and what had happened, as shocked as if they'd been in a car crash.

Emily stopped in the middle of the pavement.

'Right, we need to eat.'

'But we just had breakfast,' Tarkus said.

'It's like you never heard of second breakfast.' She shot him some side-eye. 'You know fear makes me hungry, and that was terrifying.'

Five minutes later they were sat on a bench by Regent's Canal with syrup and pancakes (in that ratio) for Emily, and a bunch of cheap flowers for Tarkus to chew.

He glanced with concern at the takeaway coffee she was holding. 'Are you sure that's advisable? Remember how you said it makes you "jabbery".'

'I need full brain speed for this.' She took a big swig and grimaced at the sour taste. 'Right, that was intense. What's she up to and what can we do about it?'

'The Nocturne claims to have almost completed a scheme to bring about both the fall of her sisters and the Great Working, and has plans to personally murder you.' He tallied the unpleasant details on his fingers.

'It won't be a claim.'

'I'm sorry?'

'She doesn't lie. If she said it, it's true. Something terrible *is* happening.'

Tarkus's already grim expression darkened.

'Then it is imperative we return to the Hour and warn her sisters of the threat.'

'We can't until midnight though,' said Emily. 'Stupid blooming spell! We don't even know what the threat is either.'

'It is something sent from your past, according to her.' He narrowed his eyes. 'And your cousin altered the clock to make it happen, to make all the time shadows happen. She practically admitted it.'

'She had a bad penny too, I saw it. She must be using that somehow.' Emily scrunched her face up in frustration.

'Argh, it's driving me mad, we can't just sit here.' She jumped to her feet, sloshing coffee everywhere. 'What if we got back in the clock and put my bad pennies on the pendulum?'

'Know a lot about fixing giant magic clocks, do ya?' Tarkus said, in a cruel parody of her accent. She gave him extreme death-squint, but he had a point. 'I fear that could be like putting kerosene on a fire.' He shook his head. 'We wish to fix it, not break it entirely.'

'Argh. Fine. You're probably right.' She took another big swig of coffee, and followed it with a mouthful of pancake. 'There must be something though. There's always something!' she said, through the food. He reached out and gently took the coffee cup from her.

'You're vibrating, you've probably had enough,' he said. 'I share your frustration, but the blood is spilt and the dragon already bolted.' He smelt the coffee, grimaced and tipped it on to the grass. 'I don't see that there's anything we can do but wait.'

She sat back down next to him with a gusty sigh. 'Man, that is extraordinarily heavy.'

'Indeed.' He sat in a fug of wet bracken smell. 'Empty time is salt in the wound of worry.'

'Don't you start quoting as well.'

'Just my mother, not a book.' He frowned so hard his smooth skin wrinkled up. 'I am worrying about more than just this awfulness. I fear the Library was too dismissive of the MBDA threat.'

'You reckon?'

He nodded. 'Neither of you have seen them like I have, their vileness. Their belief is strong and fuelled by fear.' He covered his face with both hands and rubbed at his temples. 'How much worse will the fear be after the Nocturne completes her plan?'

'The Library's super powerful though . . . right?'

'If she still stands.' He looked bleak and drawn, and it wasn't just the outside atmosphere.

Her face wrinkled up in an uber-frown. 'Man, it's going to be a long day.'

It was a very long day indeed. Despite the manifold attractions of modern London, neither of them could bear to have fun while the world might be on fire, so they simply drifted from place to place. Tarkus worrying in a dark obsessive loop about what might be happening at home, and Emily lurching in a guilty spiral as to whether she should call her parents or not. If moral wrestling had been an Olympic event, Emily reckoned she'd have been up for a medal. It was late in the evening when she finally cracked it.

'So, if I get in touch, they'll try and stop me, guaranteed, but they do need to know what's going on, so . . . here's the solution!'

She waved a handful of bright images of London at him.

'Postcards?'

'Postcards!'

He shook his head.

'I agree you must return, but I fear you are postponing a terrible reckoning,' he said. 'Your mother may actually be scarier than mine, and I do not say that lightly.'

'She'll totally understand,' said Emily, who knew she wouldn't. She scribbled furiously on her lap, from their seat on a bench at the top of Primrose Hill. The lights of the city spread out before them like a bed of gleaming flowers. Tarkus looked at his night watch.

'We have only an hour or two left.'

'Thank god! Right, the Library said to meet her at Paternoster Row. I'll take us the scenic route.'

Later, they climbed up the gentle incline from the river, the familiar sight of the dome of St Paul's cresting above the buildings. Emily joined Tarkus under the shimmering shadow of the nightshade to escape a sudden rain shower. They stepped out on to Ludgate Hill, gawped as the cathedral revealed itself in all its majesty, then gasped as something else entirely caught their eye.

From the small curve of trees to the left of St Paul's, a huge deer, big as a horse, thick with muscle and dark russet fur, strode out into the road. Seated on its wide back, knees curled in front of her and wearing a gown of emerald moss, was a woman of regal bearing. She had long white hair dappled with fawn spots, skin brown as bark, eyes as green as leaves, and a broad set of antlers jutting from her temples. The Antler Lady was frowning and looking up and down the street, raising her head to sniff the air. Where the giant deer stepped, moss and wildflowers grew in its path. The few cars that were still on the city streets just drove calmly around them. No one screeched to a halt and got out with a phone, or shouted 'Deer!', or did any of the things one would normally expect to happen. Magic was clearly afoot. (Or ahoof, in this case.)

'Aw man,' said Emily, 'I'm kind of at peak unexpected manifestation for the day already.'

Tarkus had frozen at her side, staring. 'It cannot be,' he whispered.

Emily sighed then strode forward, even as Tarkus grabbed for her arm. He missed her but she stopped anyway. The Antler Lady had disappeared, deer and all. As Tarkus caught up with her and the nightshade covered her with its magic again, the Antler Lady and her steed reappeared and continued their stately progress up the street.

'*Oh*, we can't see her without—'

'Magic, yes,' said Tarkus, tightly gripping her arm. 'She is, I think, of a lineage supposedly long vanished from the world, the Ancient Powers.'

Around the approaching duo, Emily could see the faint hazy shapes of trees. It was like they were in two places at once.

'She is of those that came before all, the children of nature that laid down the great and ancient laws.' He shook his head in wonder. 'We must let her pass unhindered.'

'But—'

'No buts,' said Tarkus firmly.

The clop of hooves on tarmac continued. The Antler Lady didn't even look their way as she drew near. Emily could smell a clear note of pine and snow, as if she was in the deep forest. Next to her, Tarkus had closed his eyes and was whispering words under his breath in a language she didn't recognize. As the lady drew level, Emily could see that her antlers were covered in soft, silvered velvet.

'Erm, hello, you're magic, yeah? How are you doing magic out here? Is it a magic reindeer? Is it like Santa?'

As she spoke, a deep aggrieved sigh came from Tarkus. It was a factor five on his sigh scale and only normally matched by very disappointed hippos as they slid back underwater.

The deer slowed and flicked an ear. The antlered head of its rider tilted towards them.

'My magic is not that of man, or of the folk. It is of the trees and the wind and the earth,' said the Antler Lady, and her voice was that very wind in the branches.

'But there's no magic left here, how does that work?' said Emily, even as Tarkus insistently squeezed her arm so tightly it hurt.

The lady's eyes were solid green, the colour of oak leaves, and impossibly deep. Emily shivered as their gazes met. She had been very sassy towards pretty seriously scary types before, but under those eyes she couldn't even dream of firing up the gob. The gaze made her want to fall asleep in a glade and think about the lady for ever. Why had she thought it was a good idea to talk to her?

'No magic?' The lady tossed her head back and laughed, and it was stream water trilling on stones. 'You think all magic is locked in your funny little box of frozen time?'

She slid from the back of the deer in one liquid move-ment. She was a lot taller than Emily had thought. Tarkus gasped beside her.

The Antler Lady bent down, her antlered head swaying, and ran her clawed fingers through the dew-silvered grass that had grown around them while they spoke. She held out a handful of grass, soil and what looked to be fallen acorns, her green eyes glowing like emeralds.

'My kind's magic lives in this. We keep the laws, make the mountains grow and the sun rise.'

The air around Emily felt different, full of the joy of a spring day. Even being near the Antler Lady was like taking a step into another world.

'I have been here since this all was trees.' The Antler Lady smiled. 'And I will be here after you are all gone, when all this is trees again.'

'Oh,' said Emily.

'Now,' said the Antler Lady, putting the handful of grass and moss into Emily's hand, 'I have indulged you, Pooka, because your kind and mine have oft been friends. And yours too, quiet little ghûl, far from your hills. But this audience is over.'

She remounted her deer, and looked around once more. 'I came only because, amongst the strange ripples in time caused by whatever foolishness you're up to now –' she frowned, as dark as a badger's den – 'I thought I sensed an old friend's presence nearby. A friend I haven't seen since Diana's temple stood upon this hill.' She shook her head, her antlers' velvet fur gleaming. 'But there is nothing here, and I care not for all the rest of your kind's greed and waste.'

And then, without a backward glance, the lady and the deer twisted sideways and stepped into somewhere that wasn't there and were gone. Emily had a confused impression of a deep green forest and a smell of sylvan air.

'What on earth just happened?' she said, looking at the

palmful of soil and greenery she'd been left with.

'I . . . I've never smelt anything like that before.'

Tarkus was stock-still, awestruck, nostrils flared as he scented the air. The moment was broken by a cab violently blowing its horn at them. They were standing in the middle of the road.

As they scrambled to the kerb, there was a ferocious bout of scratching, meeping and movement from Emily's satchel. Opening it, she was surprised when the Hog, wide awake and bright-eyed, surged out over her hands, then down her leg and out into the street. It was as fast as she'd ever seen him move. He sniffed in wide circles around the green moss that still covered the road, and made a weird barking grunt noise in his throat as he did. Emily made a dive to save him from certain death in the traffic, and his little paws and underbelly were wet and cold on her hand. His back legs kicked in the air and he snuffled and snorted and sniffed at the fading scent of forest green.

'I'm glad you're awake, you ridiculous spikeball. We will discuss this curious behaviour at your next review.'

She kissed his little black nose and slid him back into the satchel. There was going to be no pocket hedgehogging with these jeans on.

'Right, come on, Spock, it's nearly midnight, let's get you back home to Vulcan.'

'I resent that, despite not knowing what it means,' said Tarkus, his pointed ears tucked snugly under his beanie.

'And you needn't think I'm letting "quiet little ghûl" pass un-mocked. I'm just biding my time.'

CHAPTER 12

As soon as they stepped back into the moonlight of the Midnight Hour, Emily knew something was very wrong.

The full moon still burnt in the sky with its old cold flame, but it wasn't alone now. There were shapes silhouetted against it. They were not the vast angular ghosts of modern buildings that had floated there before. These were new, different time shadows, smaller but more numerous, like a pod of malformed whales bobbing all over the sky. Spotlights scanned across them, revealing them to be vast dun-coloured canvas balloons, all rigged with ropes. *Wait, spotlights?* They didn't even have those here.

Emily knew she recognized all this from somewhere, but where?

Then a sound came that made all her memories click into place. It was a rising and falling wail, loud enough to cut through sleep, loud enough to kick a city from its beds. It was a moaning, groaning scream that sounded like raw fear. She'd only ever heard it before in films and history lessons. It was the sound of air-raid sirens, and the shapes above them were barrage balloons tethered to protect London from aerial attack. Now she could hear something else, something worse, the growl of aircraft engines above and the whistling howl of the dreadful things they were dropping on to the city.

The Nocturne had told the truth. She had found something terrible out of London's history to send into the Midnight Hour. This was the final adjustment. These were the worst days London ever faced. This was the Blitz and death was in the sky above them.

'What's happening?' gasped Tarkus, hurriedly fixing his big beard back on.

'Something really really bad,' she said. 'This is a war that happened a long time ago for me, but it's in your future. And they've got planes, flying machines, and they're bombing...'

She broke off, another faded memory from her history lessons lighting up flame-bright in her head.

'Oh god, this is what the Nocturne meant. These bombs burnt Paternoster Row to the ground. It was one of the worst fires in the whole Blitz.'

'But the Library!' said Tarkus, and then they were both running.

They had to fight their way through streets clogged by hordes of frightened Night Folk, tentacles waving, wands flashing, eyes agleam with fear at this new terrible apparition roaring above them. As they ducked under the arch of the covered passageway that led to the quiet, steep-sided street of magic bookshops that Emily loved, there was a thunderous explosion from the other side that blasted a hot hurricane of dust into the passage and knocked them both off their feet.

Tarkus pulled Emily up. He was covered in grey dust and his fake beard had been blown off, and now dangled from one ear. It would have looked hilarious if it wasn't for the single bead of blood carving a wet path through the dust on his face. Emily looked down to find herself just as grey as he was. They patted at each other to be sure they were all still there, pointing and mouthing words as their hearing slowly hummed back up from nothing. Emily ripped her bag open to check the Hog and found him soundly asleep and undisturbed. Typical. Assured of each other's intactness, they staggered on through the archway, which was now filled with hanging clouds of dust and rubble underfoot.

Stepping on to Paternoster Row revealed a scene that Emily didn't think she'd ever forget, even though she'd wish she could. Paternoster Row was the single street where every publisher and bookseller in Midnight London set out their wares. The narrow street was lined with shopfront after shopfront, all with stalls set outside too, and every window and table was filled with books. Not just normal books either, but magic books. They usually flew and swooped and murmurated like flocks of starlings, and were one of the wonders of Midnight London. But it was different now.

Bombs had reduced half the buildings to piles of crushed bricks and glass and paper, as if they'd been flattened by a bored giant. But these had been incendiary bombs, intended to burn as well as explode, and there could be no worse place for them to have landed. The street was ablaze. Fire raged everywhere Emily looked, fire that leapt and hopped and raced from place to place, from spilt tables of books in through shattered windows to roar through shelf after shelf. Blazing through a lifetime's reading in moments and alphabetical order.

Paternoster Row burnt and the flock of magical books burnt with it. They still flew, but now, set alight by the ever-hungry flames, madness drove them to flap, thump and collide, to swoop, crash and burst, spilling their pages on to the dust of the street. The air was no longer full of the dry sweep of papered wings; now it was a screeching hiss, as old leather bindings ignited like kindling. The books burnt in the air, a flock of flame-winged birds spreading the fire even further in their agonies. Desperate book merchants wept in the street as they looked up to see their whole world burning.

'Oh god, Tarkus, this is terrible.' She looked at the remains of the street that had become so dear to her, at the signs the bookshops had in place of numbers, most gone in the first blast, and some crumbling in the raging flames.

'Tarkus, the Library was supposed to meet us here. Do you think she . . . ?'

They stumbled up the street, mouths covered against the dust and smoke. Their usual shop to meet in, 'D. Read & Co', simply wasn't there anymore. It was nothing but shattered stone and a roaring bonfire of books blown out of the front window by the blast. Paper fluttered everywhere, little ribbons of words, charred and adrift on the wind.

'What if she was in there?' Emily sobbed out.

Tarkus said nothing, just swayed and smeared blood across his cheek with trembling fingers.

The fires raged around them – it was getting hotter and hotter in the thin street of tall buildings, the wind and the crazed flying flaming books driving the raging fire to become an inferno. All around them came the steady thud of burnt-out books plummeting from the sky and smashing into the street.

'We have to go,' Tarkus said, and pulled at Emily's arm.

'But, what if she—'

'It's not safe to stay here.' He guided her away, slapping at burning blots of ashen paper as they sifted down, scorching hair and skin and clothes.

Ahead of them the super-heated air created a small whirlwind of smoke and burning paper. All the charred books on the ground around it sprang open and their pages began to flick over, darkness streaming from them into the growing whirlwind. It was pulling the very words and ink from the books, their scorched pages turning blank. The inked cloud swirled and roiled and then reality stuttered, like the whole world had blinked, and the Library was there.

Or at least, partly there. She towered above them as she reared up, but Emily could see through her to the blazing street behind. Translucent as a sheet of tracing paper, her long black hair wrapped around her like a mourning cloak, her eyes, mouth and nails ink-dark and wet, spilling trails like black blood as she swayed. She threw back her head and screamed. The Library *was* books and now the very words that made her were burning away.

Emily had barely started to reach out to her when there was another blink in reality, and the Library was right in front of her, grabbing at her with long-fingered hands, bending down to put her face close to Emily's.

'*He who destroys a good book, kills reason itself!*' she screeched, as tears of black ink streamed out of her eyes and inky bile ran from her mouth, cascading from her chin down her chest. She had never looked less human. Emily grabbed for her hands, but she was gone. Reality blinked and blinked and the Library moved away from them in leaps, not passing through the spaces in between. She screamed and writhed in agony, her body wracked with convulsions as she moved deeper into the fires.

Emily tried to run after her but was held back by Tarkus.

'You cannot follow her in there,' he said.

'But she's hurting!' she shouted.

He shook his head, eyes gleaming with tears.

'It is beyond us. This has struck at the very heart of her.'

The flaming books that flew madly above became even more agitated at the Library's presence, crashing and rolling and trying to reach her. She was on her knees now, sunk into the waving cloak of her long black hair, and so see-through that the rubble on the street was visible through her legs where they curled beneath her. She looked up at Emily from within the fire and her eyes were white again, as if all the ink had run out of her.

'And after the fire a still small voice,' she said, quite clearly over the bedlam around her.

'Oh, Booky,' Emily sobbed.

The Library's eyes shone now, but it was with the light of the fire leaching through her from behind, burning up all that she was.

'Protect my sister. Protect Art, for I am undone,' she said and the words sounded directly in Emily's ear. Then the Library shivered and the lines of her blurred to the black of ink, which became words, innumerable words that hovered on the air for a moment then dissolved, and she was gone.

Above them the burning magic books of Paternoster Row flew in swirling formation one last time. They gathered above their fallen mistress, in all their remaining numbers, spiralling up, up, up – a tower weaved from fiery flight. At the peak of their arc they burst into a million blazing fragments and sifted back down to earth as ash.

There would be no more books in this street, no more words; it was no longer home to the truth, for Language was dead.

Tarkus half marched, half carried a sobbing Emily away from the roaring inferno. Everywhere around them fire lit the streets, and howls, sirens and the thrum of bombers above filled the night. The grand old magnificence of St Paul's itself had been hit and flames flickered about the slates, but still it stood proud above the smoke. The lengthy whistle of a falling bomb followed by the inevitable pavement-shuddering explosion became commonplace, but never less terrifying.

They walked numbly, unspeaking, leaning on each other, moving with crowds of Night Folk making the same shambling progress. The folk had been unearthed from bedchambers and parlours, chophouses and gambling clubs, from covens and towers, and nests and lairs. They all trudged down the street together: goblins and ogres, naiads and dryads, boojums and creepers, door trolls and hippogriffs. The Night Folk of London, pushed together by common misfortune, shuffling and limping, penny-farthing riding and goat-hopping, towards a safety they weren't even sure existed.

Emily was moving through a nightmare. She'd watched the Library dissolve, seen her die. Her head and ears were still ringing from the blast, while all around them was a tramping convoy of sad, scared people saying uglier and uglier things. Things that made Emily not want to be here, or even to help them at all.

In every conversation that Emily overheard there was a common thread. That this wouldn't have happened in the old nights, the good old nights. When things had been better, before the clock, before the spell. Before, before, *before*, back when they were great. This was an attack from the Daylight and someone needed to show them who the boss was. The only way to put it right was firm leadership, an iron hand, and to start the blinking clock. Start the clock and seize the night and Make Britain Dark Again.

The river gleamed in the moonlight ahead. Dragged by the madding crowd, they were heading over London Bridge to the other side of the river, where no fires or strange flying things could be seen. Emily tugged at Tarkus's arm and pulled his head down to hiss urgently in his ear.

'You heard the Library, we need to protect Art,' she said, face tight. 'We need to get to the Great Working and away from this lot.'

He saw the look of anger on her face. He'd heard the same things she had.

'They are scared, and fear can make you angry.'

'Whatever. Come on, Art's all on her own, and not even awake.' She bounced on her heels. 'We have to hurry.'

Suddenly a commotion began behind them. Even with the air raid and sheer press of people, the shouting and booing and screaming grew too loud to ignore.

'Tarkus, what's going on?'

He shrugged helplessly, unable to see over the crowd. Emily grabbed hold of a nearby iron lamp post and hauled herself up. Something or some things were forcing their way through the crowd. They weren't tall or she'd have seen them, but she saw people jump into the air, or hurl themselves out the way, cursing and screaming. Where they passed they left ugly angry faces, raised fists and words shouted with fear and disgust. She couldn't make it out at first, then, as the invisible blades cutting through the crowd got closer, the cries of outrage became clear.

'Cursed beasts! Traitors to all!'

'Damn them! Damn the Pooka!'

CHAPTER 13

'Pooka! Filthy Pooka!'

To hear her people's name shouted with such violence made Emily's heart both leap and sink at the same time. Massive black hounds with red eyes burst through the crowd, while black hares leapt from between people's feet. The black tide of Pooka flowed like a wave towards her, crested by a huge white hound, more wolf than dog. With the hiss of steam escaping a train boiler, the white hound transformed into a craggy old lady, with long white hair, a black eyepatch and a huge fur coat.

'Mammy Espeth!' shouted Emily. She leapt into a gruff hug and bristly kiss on the forehead.

'Finally!' said Mammy. 'I've been trying to track ye down since I smelt ye by the Night Post!'

'We've been outside in my world, and— Oh Mammy!' Her lip trembled. 'Art's in trouble and the Library's . . . gone.'

Mammy's frown deepened. 'Aye, I felt it.' She gripped Emily's shoulder. 'Look, tell me all later. They're already on our tails, we need to go.'

'Who's they?' Emily asked, confused. The question was answered as a sound cut through the din of the air raid. It was a sound Emily knew she'd never forget, the brassy bugling screech of a hunting horn. It was the Hunt in full cry, but there was something new mixed in with it, a terrible rock-gargling roar of pure hunger.

Emily's stomach did an involuntary cartwheel.

'Oh dear god, is that the Bear?'

The Bear, the Nocturne's right-hand mammal, half a ton of teeth, claws and fur, who had nearly eaten her more times than she liked to think about. Really not good news.

'Aye, he's their new bloodhound.' Mammy nodded grimly. 'Can ye change?'

'Erm, yes, but hound's probably best, I haven't quite managed the horse yet.'

Mammy raised an eyebrow but nodded. 'Polis-man,' she barked at Tarkus, who jerked to attention. 'Ye'll ride with Donal.'

One of the hounds turned into a sour-looking, muscled chap with long hair and a leather waistcoat.

'And Donal – don't try and drown him in a lake. We've talked about this,' said Mammy.

The horns and the hideous howling of the were-bear sounded dangerously close now.

'It's time. We've got to go!' shouted Mammy to the clan at large, and with the *paff* of a dove coming out of a magician's hat, she was her great hound self again. Emily and Tarkus exchanged a quick nervous glance, then Tarkus climbed on to Donal, now a vicious-looking black stallion. Emily reached deep inside and pulled her hound form over herself. She transformed, her human self and all her possessions sliding into the void of cosmic laundry space with only an odd drag from her satchel, which felt like it might contain all the rocks from Stonehenge. She landed on all four feet, and stretched her long back. Her hound form had improved, from a little old lady's terrier to a big shaggy grey dog. The sort of dog you'd let finish your crisps in the pub garden (as she'd happily proved).

With growls and barks and mad whinnying, the Pooka clan charged forward. Emily ran with them, red-eyed and fleet-footed. The combined pack of horse, hound and hare bounded across the bridge and through the crowd, who shouted horrible things but were far too scared of the infamous Pooka bad-luck curse to do more. Tarkus leant forward like a jockey, knees tucked in and moving with Donal's every stride. All that recent practice with Painty was coming in handy.

Midnight London flooded in through Emily's new nose. It smelt of terror, smoke and fire. Behind them was a different smell though, one of rotting flesh, stale blood and the stench of wyrm slime. It was the reek of the Hunt. They were the Dead, and their only purpose was death.

Emily knew she should be worrying about getting away, and her hound self gloried in the running, but as the clan followed Mammy east, away from the Great Working, she couldn't escape the feeling that she was doing the wrong thing. How was she going to keep her final promise to the Library and protect Art? With the horns of the Hunt blowing behind them, it seemed impossible.

She risked a look back over her shoulder and the Hunt was there, baying at their heels. In front, a wave of the awful hunting hands, the size of big dogs, bounding forwards on their fingertips like leaping spiders. Behind came the hunters, mounted on the great black wyrms, awful slug-serpents with the long thin snouts of dragons. The riders were masked in gold, grotesque fanged faces carved on to their armoured visors, sharp silver lances in their hands. Then, worst of all, emerging from the middle of the pack came a pounding mass of dark fur, huge teeth glinting in the light of the fires. The Bear. She could have sworn he met her eye in that moment, and roared all the louder.

She put her head down and ran for all she was worth. Her four paws barely touched the ground, tongue lolling out of her mouth, sides heaving like a bellows. The sounds from behind were awful and getting closer. The scritch of nails on stone, the waterfall slither of the wyrms' slimy bellies, the terrible rumbling bassline of the Bear. Emily was starting to despair of getting away when a big surge of energy flew past her, like a horizontal lightning bolt – Mammy had used her powers to push some bad luck on to their pursuers.

Behind them, a hippogriff that had been pulling a bloodman's cart took fright and went wild. It bucked and backed and tipped the whole cart over in the road, shattering blood bottles and spilling red sticky stuff everywhere. The Bear cannoned into the cart at top speed, followed by the pack of hunting hands, their jagged fingernails slipping on the wet cobbles like deer on ice. A ghastly pile-up formed as the speeding wyrms slammed into them from behind. The already very upset hippogriff laid about itself with its sharp beak and chaos reigned.

For a moment, the Pookas' lead lengthened, probably enough to make a clean getaway, but Emily couldn't just keep running away. Not when Art needed her. Looking ahead down the river, she saw a way to keep her promise, and a plan was born complete in her mind.

She ran furiously until she drew level with Mammy's massive white form, then overtook her as the clan matriarch's ears shot back in surprise. The surprise turned into shock when Emily cut across in front of her, barking furiously, and headed off towards the river on their left. Dogs couldn't talk, but she could only hope that the message to follow her was obvious enough.

Her destination towered out of the night above them, and a swift glance showed Mammy following her, with the whole Pooka clan on her tail. Mammy didn't look very happy, but Emily figured she'd worry about that if she managed not to die in the next five minutes.

They passed great beams of blue-painted iron and ran under a broad stone arch that spanned the road. Then suddenly there was water on both sides below them. Above, a great castellated tower of pale grey stone, topped with great spires capped in gold. They were on Tower Bridge, and as they ran the entire structure flickered strangely in the darkness, like a silent movie. It was a time shadow, yet to be built and not truly of this world.

With Emily at their head, the Pooka hurtled across the shimmering bridge, the Thames silver below them. They cleared the second shadowy tower, racing through the arches and out the other side. As soon as they had crossed the river, Emily slammed the brakes on and turned back into human form. The change and the exhaustion made her want to fall to her knees, but she simply didn't have time. She'd nearly caused a full clan pile-up, and there were howls and whinnies of outrage. With the hiss of an overboiled kettle, Mammy changed back too.

'Whut's with ye?' she shouted, wild-eyed. 'Are ye sickening? I'll give ye a lift—'

'No,' said Emily, panting, 'but we can't just run and hide. We need to get to Art. Now.'

Mammy was shaking her head in disbelief.

'We've already lost family to these devils, I'll not lose more.'

'I know,' said Emily. 'We're going to deal with them first, then go straight to Art.'

'Errr, Emily,' said Tarkus from atop Donal's back, as the horns of the Hunt blared out across the river. They'd cleared the roadblock and weren't far behind.

'There's no time. Ye'll come with us or I'll knock ye out an carry ye,' said Mammy.

Around her the clan were shuffling their paws and hooves, like they were stood on too-hot sand.

Emily pointed in the direction the Hunt were coming from. 'I've got a plan,' she said. 'They're not chasing us now, you see.'

'Oh they definitely are, ye mad baggage,' said Mammy, even her unflappable calm starting to fray.

'No, I've *led them here*. That's different. Listen . . .'

And she told them, rapidly, the plan that had materialized in her brain moments ago – the brain that, just sometimes, could put things together in patterns that other people couldn't. It was simple enough (the plan, not her brain). She tugged the bad pennies out from under her shirt to prove she could do it too.

The Pooka all looked at Mammy, who was stone-faced.

'It's fierce dangerous and will probably go horribly wrong.' She wheeled on the clan, grinning. 'I like it. We're doing it.'

The howl of the horns was close enough to vibrate teeth now.

Behind them Emily could hear the awful scratch and thump of the hands hitting the roadway of the bridge. The pack of hands and two of the fastest wyrm riders were already scratching and sliming their way across it. At the head of them, the Bear. He reared to his hind legs and shambled forward, nearly ten foot tall and drool dripping from his fangs. His roar echoed from the ironwork of the bridge. They'd never get away now. If she'd got this wrong, she'd killed them all.

She gripped the jangling mass of the bad pennies, then closed her eyes and reached for them with her Pooka luck sense. She went deep into the pennies, the unluckiest, most cursed coins in the world, to see what they held. It was almost too much for her. Luck like lightning, a vast crackling maelstrom of ill-fortune. She couldn't hold it or she'd just burn away, but she could act as the pivot that helped it move.

She let it slide through her without touching it. Not all of it, for surely that might break the world, but still a huge thunderbolt. She made a ball of power and pain, until she was so full of ill-luck her hair was standing on end and she thought she might explode. She opened her eyes to see the Bear and the whole of the Hunt thundering through the arch under the second tower, screaming murder and ready to slaughter them all. Emily just smiled and, using the oldest power of the Pooka, she pushed her luck.

The biggest ball of ill-fortune that had ever been moved by Pooka hands crashed into the Hunt like a tidal wave. For a second, nothing happened. The hands were halfway across the final span and poised to leap. The Bear was lumbering into a charge. The foremost wyrm rider had a lance levelled right at Emily's heart and was screaming something vile. Then the unluckiest thing that could possibly happen . . . did.

Tower Bridge vanished. It wasn't from this time, was only here at all because of Bron's magical manipulations. It vanished just as Tarkus had told her it had been doing 'occasionally' ever since it had appeared. After all, what was the most unlucky thing that could possibly happen to a hunt crossing an occasional bridge to catch their worst enemy?

The bridge disappeared under them, popping out of existence as simply as a soap bubble. The Bear yowled a high-pitched shriek as he fell into the deep, dark, fast water far below. The hands looked like they were running in place for a moment before they plunged into the Thames. The wyrms writhed and thrashed as they fell, their riders barely having a chance to scream. Down and down they all plummeted into the river, before vanishing.

Emily grinned, then threw up and passed out. Only for a second, though, and Mammy caught her before she landed in her own sick, so that was good. She felt really very dodgy indeed.

'Yer lucky yer brains didn't come out of yer ears,' Mammy growled. Her eye softened as the rest of the Pooka whooped and hollered around them. 'Still, not a bad job. I was hoping for a kraken, mind.'

Emily stared at the absence where the bridge had been. *Yeah, bridges shouldn't be occasional.* It was disturbing. She spied movement on the other bank. A glint of black and gold, and paler things too.

'Damn it, we didn't get them all.'

'I'll finish the job with me teeth later. We owe them more than a swim.' Mammy paused, her face dark. 'There's sumthin ye should know. Yer uncle Patrick, he's . . .'

Mammy's face crumpled. 'He's missing. We don't know. He got hunted, that's known, and he hasn't come back yet.'

Emily's heart stopped.

'He'll probably turn up. He always does.' Mammy tried to grin, but it was a struggle. 'The gods protect fools, drunkards and the Irish, so that boy is triply covered.'

Emily reached over and squeezed Mammy's hand. They shared a look but neither spoke. They didn't need to.

'We need to get to Art, now. We have to protect her.'

Mammy eyed her. 'Can ye run?'

Emily answered by changing. She was weak but fuelled with rage at the fate of her loved ones. This time she transformed into a hulking grey wolf of a hound, and bared her teeth in fury.

Then they were off, running back west along the Thames, through the fires and the bombs and the hell that had been brought to this midnight sanctuary, to reach the one remaining person who could keep the clock from chiming Midnight.

They ran to protect Art, and save the world.

CHAPTER 14

The clan ran hell for leather, pell-mell and devil-catch-the-hindmost along the sweeping silver curve of the Thames. They ran to reach Art and keep her safe inside the clock that held the world. They ran as bombs tumbled from the sky, fire and shrapnel bloomed across the street like deadly flowers, and the city screamed. It would be recorded as one of the legendary rides of the Pooka clan.

But they were still too late.

As they cleared the grand avenue of Whitehall, with the great spire-coroneted tower of Westminster dead ahead, the clock tower stood out bright in the night to their left, wreathed in emerald light. A brief second of relief was shattered as Emily saw the huge crowd that filled the whole of the road and Parliament Square beyond. It was an impassable wall of people.

'What in the Morrigan's knickers is going on?' Mammy gasped as she changed back to her human form.

The noise of the crowd was colossal, a roar that reminded Emily of the thrum of football crowds when she'd walked past the stadium on match day. It wasn't just raw noise though, there were words in there too.

'Start the clock! Start the clock!'

'Make Britain Dark Again!'

The crowd jeered and cheered and held placards with bold writing on:

It's Time to Chime!

MAKE THE CLOCKWORK *WORK*

It's Not Wrong to Bong

There were crudely drawn pictures of a shattered clock tower. All eyes were fixed on the giant Roman candle that was the Great Working, the very spell that held them all safe here. The crowd had come to demand it be destroyed, to do it themselves if need be, it seemed. This was the fear and anger Emily had witnessed earlier, but brewed up now into hate, a hate that had spread amongst the Night Folk like fire had spread through Paternoster Row. How had it happened so fast?

'How can they even think this?' she shouted at Tarkus. 'It won't work. They can't take the dark with them!'

'They've been fed lies and hope.' Tarkus shrugged helplessly. 'And hope might be the more dangerous of the two.'

'This is *her*, isn't it?' said Emily with a chill as the picture came together in her head. 'The Bear was with the Hunt. The whole MBDA thing was the Nocturne all along.'

'This is her final adjustment.' Tarkus nodded, face stiff with horror. 'Your Blitz was just the match. This is the true fire.'

Emily grabbed Tarkus's arm and yelled in his ear. 'We need to get to Art now!'

'Emily,' said Mammy urgently, but she was already plunging into the crowd with Tarkus. The path through was a nightmare. These were people buoyed up with the fierce joy of righteous anger, with someone else to blame and fingers to point. It filled them with a hot boisterous energy, and they bounced and shoved and elbowed, whipping each other up further into ferment.

She lost sight of Tarkus in moments. She was crushed and pushed, and took a blow to the side of her head that left her ear a mass of red pain. The crowd was one huge beast that, if it rolled the wrong way, could crush her dead. It tugged and pulled at her, writing pain in blue and purple ink all over her as she moved through. Her only advantage was her size. She gave herself up to the sway of the crowd, riding with it rather than pushing against it, and dived through gaps, shoved under arms and through legs, and let it carry her along.

Hellish minutes passed, then suddenly she'd broken through to a small oasis-like gap in the crowd caused by three particularly large trolls. She was only a row or so away from the front. Surrounding the tower was a thin green line of the sorcerer squad charged with the vital task of guarding the clock's mechanism. Their wand tips sparked with dangerous black light and the crowd kept their distance. Even so, the sorcerers' line had been pushed back to the very base of the tower, and they looked distinctly nervous.

How was she going to get in? There were mad people all around and a twitchy line of hair-trigger combat sorcerers ahead. It seemed like a bad time to try the 'Do you know who I am?' routine. There had to be a way though. A grunt and a thud later, the crowd spat out a battered ghûl in black leather who stumbled on to his knees near her. Tarkus's beard had gone for good and his dark glasses were cracked. She hauled him up.

'This is bad. We need to—'

Before he could say anything further, there was a great roaring disturbance from the far side of the crowd, closest to the river and Westminster Bridge. A joyous yelling overwhelmed all other noise. Something massive moved through the crowd, big enough that it could be seen over their heads. A sinuous, sliming black shape, with a gold-masked snout and a rider armoured in black and scarlet. It was the Hunt, or what was left of it. Behind the first wyrm rider, another, and another further back. The first and largest wyrm slithered and snorted its way to the front of the crowd and stopped between them and the sorcerous guard.

With a surprising grace, the rider hopped up and stood on top of his saddle with perfect balance. He faced the crowd, pulled his gold-masked helmet off and shook back a wave of blond hair to reveal the bone-pale skin, chiselled cheekbones and highborn features of deceased nobility. It was Lord Peregrine Stabville-Chest, scion of the Hungry Dead, master of the Midnight Hunt and Chief Minister of the Make Britain Dark Again party. Also the Nocturne's left-hand man, Emily's vampiric nemesis and another entry on the growing list of people who'd tried to eat her. If he was here, then this truly was the Nocturne's party, in every sense. The crowd were already wild but now they went feral, the rock trolls behind Emily and Tarkus crashing their boulder-like forms together, shaking the very earth they were standing on.

Peregrine waved and grinned and bowed and pointed

back at the crowd in a cheesy 'it's all about you' gesture. The roaring grew.

'SPEECH! SPEECH! SPEECH!'

Peregrine touched a small blue amulet at his throat, which started to glow.

'Thank you for joining me, friends.'

His voice cut through the crowd's roar, speaking directly into every ear. Emily shivered down to her toes. The last time he had talked in her ear, he'd been about to rip her throat out. He might look handsome from a distance, but up close she knew that the bone showed sallow yellow through that pale skin, his eyes were dead pools of stagnant water and his breath was rank with old blood. He wasn't a living thing, he was a vampire and one of the Dead, and he cared not for anything other than his own hunger.

'I call you friends because we are. We are united in one common enterprise. All of us in this together.'

Says the man with an inherited mausoleum mansion and a family line going back to the conquest of Moldavia, thought Emily.

'And it is together that we will triumph over our current adversity. We have been held prisoner against our will for too long, but no more.'

As he talked, the riders of the other two wyrms opened great wooden boxes strapped to their saddles. They unfolded wide horns from them, and then cranked furiously at levers in their bases, until a haunting music began to spill out. They were giant portable gramophones. The music sounded like an anthem, the sort of thing a whole country stood up for, but it was discordant and screechy and made Emily's teeth grind together. Peregrine's amulet was amplifying the music as well. It whispered over the crowd, underlining his words.

'The experts tell us that this jail will keep us safe. Does that look safe?' He pointed to the sky behind them, where barrage balloons hung and smoke from the second great fire of London threatened to blot out the moon.

'I think we've had enough of experts, enough of spell-book learning and being told what to do!'

The crowd nodded, and oohed and aahed, and in some cases swayed along with him. What was going on? Even Tarkus was looking a bit glassy-eyed. Had he just nodded? It was the blooming music! Some horrid Nocturne enchantment. She stamped sharply on Tarkus's foot and he jumped. The spell was broken. She pushed her fingers in her ears and glared at him. He understood right away and began ripping up a handkerchief to plug his ears.

With the background of hypnotic music, Peregrine talked and talked. He ranted and raved and gestured, a furious series of jutting little movements that seemed to further entrance the crowd. Spittle flew from his mouth as he talked, white against the rippling emerald power behind him. The crowd were spellbound, literally, by his every word. Emily could barely even focus on what he said, it was just a wave of awfulness. Certain snatches stood out here and there.

'. . . Back to the days when the map was black!'

'. . . Take back magical control . . .'

'. . . Daylight filth and Pooka scum conspiring . . .'

'. . . And that will lead to rivers of blood, which I think we can all agree is a good thing . . .'

As the crowd hooted and hollered their approval, Mammy and the hulking Donal appeared at her elbow.

'Girl,' Mammy said, and her eye shone red. 'We can't be here. If they spot what ye are, yer dead.'

'Mammy, I . . . none of this is even true!' Her head was spinning. 'If the Hour breaks, most of these people are dead. Why do they believe him?'

'Some of it's that music enchantment that's making my nose itch.' Mammy sniffed. 'Mostly it's because they want it to be true. He's telling them a story of how they think the world should be.'

'They're going to do something bad. We need to get in the clock and protect Art.'

Mammy just shook her head. 'Ye'd be ripped to pieces, girl. They're a mob now, and they're hungrier for blood than the vampire.' Her wrinkled face softened. 'Sometimes ye can't win, love.'

Emily's head whirred. She just needed another mad plan. She was a plan genius. She could fix this. Unlike the Library, she could still save Art, if she could only think straight.

The speech was building to some awful climax. A growing chant of 'Let it chime! Let it chime!' came in overpowering waves. Peregrine held a hand out and, as a conductor would an orchestra, brought them all to quiet. The whole crowd bristled with expectation as he milked the moment.

'It's in your claws, my friends.' He turned sideways, one hand out to his audience, the other armoured gauntlet pointing his lance straight at the clock tower. 'Will you fight like hell for what's yours?'

The silence was split by an incoherent roar of rage, full of every scrap of fear and humiliation the people had ever suffered. Peregrine waved his lance and the black flag on the end of it as the crowd charged around him towards the Great Working, inexorable as the tide. The guards, as affected by the music as any of the crowd, turned and became the head of the charge, wands crackling in hand.

Emily screamed. 'No!'

Mammy snapped, 'Donal!' and the big Pooka's arms closed around Emily like a steel trap and she was lifted thrashing and screaming off the floor. She could do nothing but watch as the ordinary Night Folk of Midnight

London stormed the clock tower of the Great Working. The tower that held the spell that held the world. That held the helpless Art.

The crowd broke like a wave at the base of the tower. Doors were smashed in and marauders ran to start the long climb up the staircase. Other figures sailed up out of the crowd to scale the tower. Some flew; there were bat wings, black feathers and the glowing sheen of faerie skin. Others climbed; simian-armed goblins and oozing shapeless shoggoths. Faster than them all, the pallid stump-topped forms of the surviving hunting hands ran straight up the side, their awful sharp nails hauling them up. They weaved in and out of the tower's blazing fog of magics. Some tumbled back to earth in an explosion of green flames, but many reached the giant clock faces, where they hammered and smashed at the glass. There was a rending and a crashing as they forced their way in, leaving black holes in the great white sheets of glass behind them.

All of a sudden, there was a pulse of energy that rippled out to fill the whole square at once. Every stained-glass window in Westminster, every statue, every portrait in the National Gallery, every single piece of art within a mile writhed. They all opened whatever their version of a mouth was to let out a single nerve-shattering scream, before blowing into smithereens of glass, stone, card and canvas. The second of the Sisters Three had fallen. Art was gone.

The crowd's shock at the sudden devastation caused a pall of silence to fall. Emily sobbed helplessly into the quiet as glass tinkled and the injured moaned. At the top of the tower, glass cracked and fell away from the great clock faces like ice calving from a glacier. For a moment nothing happened. Then, with barely a whisper, the great arcing emerald bolts of witch-light that had glowed in the fog around the clock tower since July 1859, flickered and went out. They left behind only throbbing after-images on blinking eyes.

Then, as from a great vault locked far beneath the sea, a deep and sonorous sound. A mighty rippling impact of hammer striking on bronze, and the unmistakable, haunting peal of Big Ben rang out. The clock finished the chime it had first started a century and a half ago.

The spell was broken.

The Midnight Hour had passed.

CHAPTER 15

ig Ben's chimes pealed out across Westminster, signalling the end of the Midnight Hour. The crowd erupted into a frenzy of celebration, with roars so loud they drowned out the tolling of the great bell. They had done it! Struck a blow against oppression and seized the reins of their own destiny.

This joyous celebration lasted until the twelfth midnight chime faded away and the world ended.

In the sky above Midnight London, the moon hung full, stark, and shining as it had for nearly two centuries. A polished silver coin gleaming in the velvet black of night's treasure chest. Now, that eternal presence bucked and rippled as if it were only a reflection in the ocean's waters. The very heavens heaved, and the sounds of jubilation below changed to low moans of fear. A sheet of lightning crossed from horizon to horizon and jangled every nerve in the square. Then, with a shattering crash like every thunderbolt ever rolled up into one, the sky simply tore apart.

A cosmic rent ripped straight across the blackness, and stars fritzed out like blown bulbs. The great old bone of the moon, already sick and pale with grief, was torn asunder. The night sky blew away like black silk on the wind, revealing a blazing light. An intolerable blinding whiteness that filled the world. Blackest skies turned to shrieking blue, and the lonely sadness of the moon to an angry ball of fire.

It was the Daylight and, hung in the sky, the sun.

Fire rained down on the Night Folk. Or it might as well have done for the effect the sunlight had. Not a soul here had seen Daylight for nearly two hundred years, and none of them had exactly been keen sunbathers before that. Screams of anguish filled the square as the scourging light swept through it. Even Emily, child of Daylight, was half-stunned and blinking. The fire of the unexpected sun scorched her eyes and filled her vision with black spots.

As the tide of the crowd had crashed in, now it roared out. The Night Folk ran screaming from the awful light. Emily was torn from her companions by the panicked mob. She fell and feet stamped on her calves then her back and she knew she was going to die. She clawed her way up the fur of some passing boggart, desperate to survive. The riptide of the crowd towed her past the high railings in front of the parliament buildings and she clung on to them. She could see now if she squinted, and what she could see was terrible.

They were back in the Daylight world. There were skyscrapers, billboards and cars everywhere. She was home, but Midnight London had come with her. Ripped from its sanctuary outside of time, the Midnight Hour had crashed head-on into modern London. Everywhere she looked was madness. The great historic buildings that existed in both times barely looked any different, but elsewhere the old city writhed and warped underneath the new. Glass-fronted offices blurred into blackened stone, tall steel towers swayed as beneath them unsteady wooden inns fought to come back into being. Magical Victorian London was trying to re-emerge into a city that had changed beyond recognition, and failing. She was watching the death spasms of the Midnight Hour.

'Oh my god,' moaned Emily, 'you atrocious muppets. You blew it all up.'

It wasn't just Night Folk that were running and screaming. It was a bright autumn day and the tourist hordes were out in force. These were not the sights they'd been planning to see, though. It was easy to tell them apart in the crowd. The Night Folk were clutching their eyes (or eye stalks) and had an overwhelming preference for dressing in black and wearing serious hats. The Daylight screamers wore a lot more colour, bright trainers and backpacks, and were pointing at the Night Folk as they screamed.

The Night Folk also weren't the ones holding their phones up to take pictures of the mayhem, then wailing like anguished children to find them totally melted. Magic and technology did not mix and a huge amount of magic had just been dolloped out right in the middle of London. Emily would have bet money there wasn't an un-melted microchip for miles. It sounded like every car, burglar and house alarm in town was going off because of the magic too.

Beyond the sounds of Day- and Night-Folk distress, and the discordant orchestra of alarms, Emily could hear something else now. Something bad. Sirens. *Of course.* They were in her world now, and an army of monsters had just dropped in with an appalling bang and started a terrifying riot outside the Houses of Parliament. Someone was going to notice that. Probably someone with guns.

She couldn't let the Night Folk get hurt. Yes, a bunch of them were hateful small-minded idiots and they'd brought this upon themselves, but they'd also been musically manipulated by an evil Older Power and her followers. So many other terrible things had taken place today that she needed to try and stop anything worse happening. Maybe, if she could find a police officer and explain . . . *Police.* Where was Tarkus? Where was Mammy? How was she ever going to sort this out? She took a first hesitant step back into the square with the thought of trying to do something, anything, to head off a massacre, when the sound around her changed.

All of the alarms, the sirens and even the screaming started to warp and ripple together. The horrendous discord was woven into music. It howled and shrieked, sobbed and sang and filled the sky. Every sound in the square and possibly the whole city was woven into one all-encompassing symphony. There was only one person, one Older Power that could do that.

The Nocturne was coming, and sirens sang her praise.

Credit where it was due, Emily thought, it was the dramatic entry to end all dramatic entries. As the city's sounds of distress twisted into an orchestra unparalleled, a procession parted the terrified crowd. First a writhing carpet of the pallid hunting hands, then the remaining huntsmen, visors clamped shut against the sun, on their massive black slime-gleamed wyrms. Led by Peregrine, they waved great funereal banners from their lances, all black save for a musical note picked out in silver.

Behind them came a huge dripping figure which sent Emily diving for cover behind a souvenir stall. Walking on two legs was the furry mass of the Bear, still soaking wet and slimy from his plunge into the Thames, and looking terribly angry. Beside him, a slim figure, small by comparison, in a shimmering suit of night, with a mane of red hair (such great hair) billowing in the wind. Bron.

This honour guard preceded a giant glinting black pearlescent globe, floating just off the ground. Within it swirled all the stars of the night sky, and at its heart floated a cold supernova in a dark blue dress. The Nocturne, Music, sole remaining sibling of the Sisters Three, and currently runaway favourite for the Most Self-satisfied Expression Ever award. She took in the scene of devastation and panic with avid eyes. She smiled the broadest and most genuine smile Emily had ever seen on her face.

Floating in the very centre of her magical prison, she threw her arms wide with a graceful motion. Her hands began to dance before her, fingers darting in counterpoint. The surface of the sphere rippled, a ringing note came forth, and the very air began to change.

With a shimmer like heat haze, the magic that had poured out into the Daylight world from the Midnight Hour became visible. It was all around, as far as the eye could see, hung low to the ground like a dark, sparkling mist. Slowly but irresistibly, it was drawn towards her, streams of magic running into the globe. What had spilt from the shattered Midnight world, she was claiming for her own.

As the magic flooded in, the globe filled with blackness, the Nocturne disappeared from view and even the stars went out. It became so black it looked like a hole in the universe absorbing all light. Then, with a profound throbbing resonance that Emily could feel through her feet as much as her ears, it began to change. The sphere distorted, compressing, shrinking down and folding in, until it reached the Older Power in the centre. It draped itself over her tall, elegant frame, shrouding her in Midnight. Then, with a final ripple and a single sad note of a harp, it became a heavy shimmering hooded cloak that completely covered the Nocturne apart from her hands and face.

She took one deep breath of outside air, and nodded to herself. Then she interlaced her fingers and turned her hands palm out to stretch them, like a pianist preparing to play. It looked as if she was just about to do something when, with a howl of sirens, a squeal of wheels and the throb of helicopter blades, all of the police officers and quite a lot of the armed forces in London roared into the square and dived out, pointing big black guns at everybody and shouting a lot.

The Nocturne made no sign of noticing this at all, apart

from to lift one finger. With that minute gesture came an exquisite noise, a descending arpeggio that somehow whirled all the cocking gun bolts and boot-clad feet and cries of 'hands in the air' together into the sound of the most delicate of strings being plucked. It became a noise of such beauty and sorrow that the rapidly advancing forces of justice dropped to their knees, weapons forgotten as they clutched at their hearts and tears leaked from under their gas masks on to their great big black boots.

The Nocturne returned to the task in hand. With a twirl of her fingers, the glossy cloak flooded out behind her, midnight black and ever-growing. The inky threads of escaped magic continued to stream into it, rolling in like waves on a beach. As Emily watched, the cloak grew larger, billowing up from the ground and giving the Nocturne the appearance of having great black wings as she gathered in all the remaining magic in the world for herself.

Emily wanted to run, scream, attack and hide in a hole all at once. What was she supposed to do? The world had literally ended and everything was as bad as it could be and her arch-enemy had superpowers and an army, and she didn't even know where her friends were. A sudden horrid thought led to a desperate clutching at herself, and she gave a little sob when she found that her satchel had survived. She scrabbled it open and could have cried to see the Hog in there. He was unsquashed and mainly awake, if clearly very grumpy. Twice through the cosmic laundry plus a riot was guaranteed to produce a hog in a huff. She plucked him out, and cradled him in her palm.

'Hog, what the hell are we supposed to do?' she whispered. 'They've blown the world up.' He didn't look any happier at this news. 'I can't see sarcasm and my unique personal charm fixing this one.'

She was acutely aware that pretty much everybody in the world who would like to see her dead was standing right over there. It wasn't paranoia if they really were out to get you. The Nocturne might be lost to the world in her swaying, magic-weaving reverie, but what about the Bear? His sense of smell was incredible. How long before he spotted her if she stayed? But how could she get away without being seen?

Suddenly there was a disturbance. A loud raised voice.

'Lady, Great Lady, I must speak with you.'

It was Bron. She knelt before the Nocturne as the ink-mist of magic flowed around her. If Emily was any judge, Bron looked terrified. Her face was pale and her teeth were jammed into her lip, but still she kept talking.

'Great Lady, please. This . . . this isn't what you said would happen. Many of the Night Folk have been hurt.' She looked up now, chin firm. 'My people have been hurt.'

The Nocturne slowly opened her eyes. She didn't look pleased to be disturbed. 'People always get hurt by great and necessary changes, but that was not our bond.'

Behind her, the cloak billowed and thrashed, reeling in the cindery darkness that swirled around her, growing larger all the time.

'I promised you'd be my sword. That fear and terror would be twin hounds at your side. Have I not given you this?' She nodded at the devastation around them.

'Yes, you have, and I'm grateful, but –' Bron rose and wheeled to point at the Hunt and their hunting hands – 'I have smelt these filthy things, and they stink of the blood of my people.' She lashed out with a boot at a hunting hand that had got too close. 'They have hunted them. Was that your order, Lady? Because that was not our bond.'

Bron sounded like she was begging to be told it wasn't so.

The Nocturne smiled, a delicate dinner-party smile of minor social inconvenience. 'Well, of course it was. They caused us insult at Coven Gardens. What else was I to do?'

Bron's cheeks were wet with tears now, but she kept staring straight at the Nocturne. Emily didn't like her, but she didn't doubt her bravery for one moment.

'That was my family. That was not . . . None of this is what it was supposed to be.'

'If you are not for me, Bronagh Maracth Connolly, then you are against me.' The Nocturne's face turned icy. 'This is not a good world to be my enemy in.'

The Hunt clustered closer around them, leering as the Nocturne spoke. The Bear had his head tipped on one side, as if watching a dog do an unexpected trick.

Bronagh closed her eyes just for a moment, then reopened them, her jaw set firm. 'You have taught me one thing, my lady . . . this is not a good world.'

Before anyone else could speak, she had moved. Even amongst the supernaturally speedy Pooka, Bron was fast. Right now she was lightning. In a dancer's step she was next to the Nocturne. Her hand lashed out like an arrow leaving a bow and hit the Older Power in the throat. As her hand whipped back, Emily saw there was a large, tarnished old coin tied flat across the front of her cousin's knuckles. Bron had walloped the Nocturne with a bad penny, an ill-luck charm that even the Older Power was susceptible to.

'Woah,' gasped Emily.

The Nocturne gagged and grasped at her throat, unable for a few precious moments to sing her words of command. The Bear was already swinging his razor-tipped paws at Bron, but she rolled away like he was moving in slow motion, then flipped backwards over the hunting hands to land in a crouch. As she sprang up, she produced a sharp wooden stake and stabbed the nearest huntsman right through his un-beating heart. He turned to dust and his wyrm keened its agony and went wild, tail lashing out and into the rest of the hunting hands.

Bron looked back once in anguish at the still-choking Nocturne before she changed into her huge black wolf-dog form. Then she was gone and running, long before the Nocturne regained her voice and screamed for her head at window-breaking volume.

Despite being stunned at the sheer awesome ninjaness of what she'd just witnessed, Emily could recognize a diversion when she saw one. As the forces of darkness all bumped into each other trying to get on Bron's trail, Emily legged it in the opposite direction, as fast as she could. Away from the Houses of Parliament, away from the Nocturne's ever-growing cloak of Midnight magic, and into a London she no longer recognized.

CHAPTER 16

Emily might have run for ever if her Pooka nose hadn't detected a familiar floral scent. She tried not to think about what her powers working in the daylight meant, and concentrated on homing in on the scent of her friend. She soon found Tarkus, blood streaming from a gash on his head, wobbling back towards Parliament Square.

'Oh, you are so going the wrong way, Flowers,' she said.

'I was coming to find you. I presumed you'd be in trouble.'

She looked at his head, and winced. 'What happened?'

'Riot things happened.' He shrugged. 'I lost Mammy

and the big chap in the crush. I may have passed out for a bit actually.'

'Oh, great.' She was already rummaging around her satchel, avoiding Hog prickles, for a bandage. The best she could do was her emergency pair of pants. 'Here. They're clean, honest.'

He must have been in pain as he didn't even cringe, just clapped them to the gouge in his scalp. The shimmering cinder smoke of magic swirled around their feet and was spread everywhere, a Midnight tide swept in over the whole of London.

'We really need to get out of here, Tee. Can you manage?'

'Yes. Where are we going?'

She hadn't known until he asked her, but it was suddenly completely clear.

'Like you said earlier, where we always go when there's a problem.' She pointed ahead. 'Home. My mum and dad are only in Lambeth, it's not far.'

Tarkus's face crumpled near to tears. Of course, she was an idiot. His family. His whole damn world, in fact.

'I'm sorry, dude. How can we get you home? I've got a feeling Uber isn't working right now.'

He gritted his teeth and shook his head. 'My mother is of the line of queens. She is more than capable of looking after herself.' He forced a smile. 'If I were to return to nanny her when I could be working to fix this, I would never hear the end of it.'

He stared at her, his face smeared with blood, his eyes on fire. 'And that's what we're going to do, yes? Fix this.'

'Too right.' She nodded. 'I don't know how yet, but we will.'

'That's enough for me. Shall we go while I'm still vertical?'

Crossing Lambeth Bridge revealed London's damaged heart. Both sides of the river were thronged with the iconic buildings that made up London's skyline, but something was terribly wrong with that view. The city writhed. Timbered buildings and great creaking rookeries of planks and filth fought for space with shiny offices, takeaways and twenty-four-hour corner shops. Everything fluttered and thrashed like a plastic bag caught in the wind as Midnight London clawed for purchase on this modern world it had been dumped into.

The river below heaved too, with a fleet of boats from the past: skiffs, steamers, smacks, all with foghorns blaring. Merfolk howled their gills out, while vast leviathans of the deep crested the surface, huge eyes glaring. Further up river, two giant tentacles had come out of the water and gripped the giant white circle of the London Eye like a steering wheel, to the horror of all the people in the viewing pods.

Emily had seen a lot of weird stuff in her time, but this, all this, was too much. It was okay when it was through the wardrobe, or the other side of the looking glass, but now it had followed her home and everything was as broken as could be. The bridge and the road beyond and everywhere she could see was crawling with people. The occasional Night Folk, but mainly Londoners (although they were all Londoners really, she supposed). They had the same terrible lost look that the Night Folk escaping the Blitz had worn. Clutching family and possessions to them, and staring more in shock than horror at what was happening to the previously safe space that had been their city. She kept her head down so she wouldn't have to look at it all anymore and marched as fast as she could for home.

The little row of terraced houses where Emily lived were quite modern, and the juddering outline of a row of old shops flickered over them as Emily and Tarkus approached. A skeleton in a grocer's apron peered over her hedge, clearly confused about what had happened to his emporium. At least her neighbours were used to deeply weird occurrences after having lived near her mum for so long. The garden gate opened with its usual tortured squeak and that familiar noise filled her eyes with sudden tears of relief.

The front door was ajar and a low hubbub of voices spilt out as they walked in. It looked like an explosion in a fancy-dress shop. There were Night Folk everywhere, sat on the stairs, down the hall, and all over the kitchen, with more noise coming from the living room. Daemons, grumplings, imps, wolfen, hags, even a manticore in the back hall wearing a fancy hat. There were faces she recognized from the post office but many strangers as well. They were all hollow-eyed and vacant with shock. More than a few of them were injured too.

She was used to seeing the denizens of the Hour, but not here, not in her normal(ish) family home. Victorian outfits and glowing eyes livid against the backdrop of beige kitchen units. Taloned hands and furry backsides resting on the white goods, horned heads slumped on the pine kitchen table. That stomach-churning feeling of the other world following her home reared up again, because it literally had.

'Em!' The yell cut through the hubbub and her mum was elbowing her way through the crowd at top speed. She flinched as her mum didn't even brake, just swept her up into a massive wordless hug, and squeezed and squeezed.

'Mum, you're loving me too tight. We've talked about this.'

Her mum reluctantly let go, and held her out at arm's length. Her feelings played out across her totally readable face – unabashed relief Emily was back, then stormy anger she'd gone off, then just general concern for all of their fates, then a sigh. She didn't say anything in the end, just narrowed her eyes and flicked Emily's ear with her finger.

'Ow!'

'If you're going to go and save the world, do better than a blasted feather and a postcard next time, ye banjax. Yer da's been worried sick.'

'Is he okay?' Emily said, rubbing her ear.

'Aye, he's in the shed making compost compresses for the dryads.'

She paused, looking over Emily's shoulder.

'Does yer man there know he's got pants stuck to his head?'

Tarkus was propped against the wall, green-tinged and ashen. His eyes were empty and his arms crossed tightly across his chest, as if to hold himself together. Emily's spare pants were stuck to the side of his head, glued there by the oozing blood.

'Now that's a man who needs to sit down and eat some petunias. Come on, lad,' said her mum, taking him gently by the arm. 'Emily, find yer da, get some flowers, then ye can fill us in.'

Emily squeezed past a hairy-backed minotaur who was

eyeing their pinging microwave with great suspicion and out the back door into the little green paradise of their garden. It was tiny, but her dad had filled every inch of it with veg and flowers and quiet joy. Just seeing it, still there, still growing, filled her heart up. Her dad was leaning over the compost heap, carefully packing a large dock leaf with his finest mulch. He bit his lip when he saw her, closed his eyes for a moment, then gave her a wry little smile. A pretty major emotional display for her dad.

'Hello, Puzzle. I knew you'd be okay.'

To her surprise, the sight of her lovely quiet dad in his lovely quiet garden made her burst into tears. Not just any tears, but great big howling snotty ones. She totally wasn't a crier though. It had just been a tough day. She ran and threw her arms around his waist, and sobbed into his jumper. He held her tight without saying anything, and they rocked there for a while. It all poured out in her tears, everything that had happened: the disaster, the death of her friends, and the very real knowledge that the horror wasn't over but was only getting worse. His calm made it possible. He was so calm, in fact, that he barely even flinched when she noisily blew her nose on his jumper.

'Oh man, that compost absolutely hums. You are a stinker,' she said, wiping the rest of the mess from her face on to her sleeve.

'I'm very pleased to see you too, love,' he said and

fuzzled her hair, which she was prepared to endure under the extenuating circumstances.

'Oh, Dad, it's all gone really really wrong.'

'We've heard, Puzzle,' he said. 'We opened the house for the Resistance to bring the injured to, but there's only so much we can do.'

'Oh! Tarkus is hurt and all woobly. Have you got any flowers he can eat?'

He snapped off a couple of later-blooming chrysanthemums and handed them to her.

'Come on, I want to hear what's happened to you, and your mother will spontaneously combust if I find out before she does.'

The whole of the house had become a field hospital, with Night Folk lying out on duvets and sleeping bags on the floor. There were bandaged heads and sunburnt skin and sore eyes and the same general look of shock as in the kitchen. Emily and her family sat in as quiet a corner of the living room as they could find, and her dad brought tea through and produced the luxury biscuit tin (only brought out for special occasions or magical apocalypses). The devil-baby was blessedly quiet and invisible under blankets in his baby carrier, as Emily told her mum, dad and a newly returned Japonica what had happened.

It was a difficult conversation. Telling her mum about the Library, Art and Pat was even worse than explaining why she hadn't saved the world.

'I knew, love. I knew when the Great Working failed. Art and the Library would never have let it happen if they were still standing,' said her mum. 'And I wouldn't write our Patrick off that easily.' She patted Emily's hand. 'It's a bad time. Bad things happen to people. We just need to make sure it doesn't happen to anyone else.'

And that was all she would say on the matter, but afterwards she looked older than Emily had ever noticed her being before, her face grave and seamed.

'And that's it,' Emily said, finishing with the horrors she'd seen in the square. 'I . . . I honestly don't know what we can do. The Hour's been destroyed, and all the magic has been lost.'

'*Harroom*. That's not entirely true.'

The interruption came from a large man Emily didn't know, who was filling up an armchair and holding an ice pack to his bruised face. He looked totally human and non-Night Folky apart from his mutton-chop whiskers, the tattered tweed three-piece suit he wore, and the odd fact that he had no shoes or socks on.

'If I might explain?'

That voice was very familiar. Wait, if she squinted and just looked at the general bulk and the tweed and the crazy whiskers, and imagined the voice coming out a bit more mangled by a big tongue and sharp teeth, then it was—

'Cornelius!'

'Of course,' he said, surprised.

'But you're . . .' She gestured at his general lack of wolfiness.

'Ah, yes, no full moon, you see. Changed back. Disconcerting after so long. Trousers keep falling down too.' He frowned down at his waistline. 'As I was saying. What you said, not really right at all, about the spell and the magic. Probably helps to visualize it.'

He settled back in his chair, gesturing with both hands.

'The Midnight Hour was a pond, no, a *fish tank*. It was full of preserved magic like a tank is full of water, and we were the fish in it. Yes?'

'Yes?' said Emily, who'd heard Cornelius's explanations before and was bracing herself.

'Now, the glass of the tank has been smashed!' He slammed his fist down on the arm of the chair, and the ice pack burst, pelting the pixies sitting next to him.

'All the water, the magic, has flooded out and all us fish with it, *glub glub glub* –' he made swimming gestures – 'and now this London is flooded with magic and for now we can still exist as we are, happy fishes. Did I say we were the fish in this analogy? Good.'

'Okaaay,' said Emily. Various of the adults were

exchanging confused glances, but he certainly had their attention.

'But there is no tank now.' His voice grew more solemn. 'So, the water, the magic, will soon drain away.'

He leant forward, his eyes intense.

'And then we fish, well, we will be beached and dry . . .'

He made a fish flopping gesture with his hand and then held it deathly still. The room had gone very quiet.

'Oh god,' said Emily. 'Then it's over, the Great Working is broken, and all the magic is just going to drain away.'

'Hrrrrmm, that's not what I said at all,' said Cornelius. 'Sometimes I wonder why I give these explanations when nobody properly listens to them,' he muttered to himself and began polishing his monocle.

'Cornelius!' Emily shouted.

'Ah, yes, right. Well, as I said, the Hour is gone, but the Great Working, which of course *is* the spell, is still viable.'

'What?' Emily's eyes had lit up almost as brightly as Tarkus's with a frustration so great that Cornelius wisely got on with it.

'It's the greatest magical artefact ever made. It takes more than a pitchfork in the clockwork to break the old girl.' He rubbed his bruised face regretfully. 'I should know. I was there. Couldn't stop them though. Or protect the great lady.'

A silence fell.

It was Japonica who spoke, as neither Emily nor her mum seemed able to.

'Professor Snark, are you saying it's possible to fix the Great Working?'

'Well, in theory.' He rubbed his chin thoughtfully. 'One would have to completely deactivate then reinitiate the spell at exactly the right time for that to work, though.'

'Hang on,' said Emily, 'are you telling me that the fix for the greatest sorcerous working in history is to "turn it off and on again"?'

'That's a vast simplification of an incredibly complex process which . . . Yes, I suppose I am,' admitted Cornelius.

'So if we do that, if we fix it, what happens, Cornelius? And –' she added swiftly – 'I need you to answer this in very simple language. Strictly no fish.'

The not-currently-a-werewolf stared off into left field, chewing his lip as he worked it through in his head.

'Well, if you did that, and you did it before it next chimed midnight, hmmm . . .' He was clearly struggling not to say anything about aquariums. 'Then it would start again, or more accurately *stop* again, recreating the Midnight Hour, as it was made to do, pulling all the magic back in, which—'

'Then why are we sat here?' Emily leapt to her feet along with a number of other excited types. The pixies broke out into a jig. 'We just need to get the gang and—'

'*Haroom haroom!*' The gruff coughing was nearly as ferocious as Cornelius's werewolf bark. 'Which, if you'd let me finish, is sadly impossible.'

The pixies stopped dancing.

'Why?'

'Because the Great Working's spell was originally created by Art and the Library, two of the most powerful beings in the world. It took all the magic they had, even then.'

He finished polishing his glasses and slid them back on, looking sorrowfully at the room. 'Without them, and with the magic being taken by the Nocturne or else draining away . . . I just cannot see how we'd ever have enough to get the clock started.'

He slumped back into the chair.

'But what if we could get the magic?' said Emily, staring at him. 'Could we make it work?'

'Perhaps, but time is shorter than you know.' His face was dark. 'You say the Nocturne gathers magic beneath the Great Working?'

Emily nodded.

'Then come midnight, I suspect she plans to bind that magic to herself, using the last of the clock's power.' Cornelius spoke very quietly now. 'Once she does that, it would be lost for ever.'

CHAPTER 17

'Okay, so we need to make a plan, a serious plan,' said Emily, filled with a frantic energy. 'I'm going to need crisps, hot chocolate and coloured pencils. And more biscuits. Lots more biscuits.'

'Before ye do anything, ye need to eat – proper food, not biscuits – then get cleaned up, and have a nap,' said her mum. Her dad nodded.

'A *nap*?!' said Emily, outraged. 'I'm not a toddler! Don't you dare try and cut me out of this! I'm going to make a plan and fix it!'

Her mum's face had the warning signs of an imminent gob explosion, but it was her dad who spoke.

'No, you're not a toddler. You're of the ruling line of the clan Connolly, and one of only two remaining Librarians serving a fallen liege.' The steel in his voice was a shock to the system. 'You're also dead on your feet. Running yourself into the ground because you feel guilty is just acting out. And that *is* toddler behaviour.'

There wasn't an inch of give in his expression. This must be how he looked when he was staring down monsters to deliver the post. Her face must have been a picture, because he leant over to touch her hand, and smiled a little.

'You *are* going to stand with us while we try and sort this out, and I don't want you falling over.'

'What yer da said. Now, eat a bloomin' sandwich, have a scrub, and get yer head down. That's an order, so it is,' said her mum. 'The world won't be any more monkeyed in an hour's time.'

'Yes, Mum,' said Emily, meekly.

One thumping doorstop of a ham'n'crisp sandwich later, Emily was in her room. Her beloved room. If she hadn't used up a year's worth of tears on her dad earlier, she could have cried again at the sight of it. The Abbits on the wall, Feesh, her cuddly crocodile, on the bed. Her piles of unread books. Everything sang of home and safety. She eased the Hog from satchel to sawdust-filled cardboard palace. He was still awake but very dozy and sank into the shavings to rest his eyes.

Then came the moment she'd most been looking forward to. She unbuttoned the optimistically sized jeans and gasped with relief as she was able to breathe again. They'd tattooed her waistline with an imprint of seams and studs. *Never again*, she vowed. She dived straight under the covers, dragging Feesh in with her. Her mum had mentioned something about washing, but she figured two out of three wasn't bad.

She lay back in fresh linen and trapped her Feesh's long green furry tail between her knees for comfort. Now she'd stopped long enough to think about it, she was exhausted. Like her dad had said, this nap was her duty. She closed her eyes, her whole body became heavy and . . . she was gone.

As her chainsaw snoring began, the Abbits on the wall started to spin of their own accord, without breeze or human hand. Their black glass glinted as the hares spun in their eternal chase above Emily's sleeping head and, if she'd been awake, Emily would have seen three glass noses twitch in alarm as they revolved.

It was the noise that woke her. She'd been in a deep sleep full of vivid, difficult dreams of burning books and ink-filled eyes, but the noise was enough to lure her back to waking. She lay there groggily in the late-afternoon half-light, feeling worse than if she hadn't slept at all. *What was that?* She looked up and saw the Abbits were spinning around like a propellor and whirring loudly as they did. Black glass nose to black glass tail, they spun so fast the hares blurred into each other. The noise was joined by an intense rustling as the Hog went crazy in his hog-palace. The cardboard boxes and tubes were creaking and rocking. What was going on?

Suddenly, a thud came from the ceiling. No, above it. There was something on the roof. Occasionally you could hear the patter and cooing of romancing pigeons up there, but this wasn't them. It was heavier, and scratchier. For one mad moment, her brain pictured reindeer and a sleigh. Then the scratching turned to scritching, and the noise was all too familiar. Not Santa after all. She dived out of bed and threw herself out the door and down the stairs, hurdling a gobhoblin as she went. She burst into the kitchen, where her mum was in deep conversation with Japonica and a newly arrived Hunts-by-Night.

'Hands!' Emily shouted. 'There are hunting hands on the roof!'

Everyone erupted. She saw her mum grab a bread knife and bolt for the back door. Even as she did there was a blazing flash of light from outside, accompanied by a *thoom* sound. It was a pillar of pure fire blasting up from the garden towards the roof. The flame cut off, there was a pause, then something big, black and smoking fell into the garden with a heavy thump.

Her mum had the door open in a flash and was outside, bread knife held in a very professional-looking combat grip. Emily was right behind her. On the ground was a charred and very dead (*dead-er*, Emily supposed) hunting hand. It looked like it had been barbecued. There was another, just as burnt, twitching its last in the bean patch. Standing over them in his cardie, face like stone, was her dad. He held his flaming sword, the one he used for really dangerous deliveries, the blade a bright flicker in the gathering dark of the autumn afternoon.

'. . . and stay out of my compost heap,' she heard him mutter, before he turned around.

'Oh, hello dear, sorry for the shock. We had unwanted visitors.'

There were black scorch marks up the back of the house. Emily's mum smiled at him like a love-struck teenager.

'Yer aim's getting worse.'

He grinned back, then turned to Emily and the assembled household who were all crammed into the back doorway. 'Er, Puzzle, you do know you haven't got any trousers on, yes?'

She had wondered why her knees were so cold. This was soon resolved by the full body blush of shame.

'Er, yeah, totally.' She pulled her T-shirt down with both hands as she backed towards the door. 'Ninja reactions, you know how it is.'

Five minutes later, she was properly dressed again, with an absolute commitment to pretending the no-trousers incident had never happened. With great relief, she'd slipped into her normal joggers and a warm hoodie, then pulled her big boots back on (which were, of course, *still* the best type of boots). She retrieved the Hog from his palace and slipped him into the satchel. He was much more awake after his frantic scurrying, but not in any better a mood. She looked at the Abbits, which were now quite still. What had happened there? She didn't have time to think about it right now.

Downstairs, her mum and dad were in the front hall, with the door open, looking cautiously out on to the street outside. Her dad wore his sword in a scabbard on his belt now. It looked out of place against his old brown gardening cords.

'I really don't like it,' he said.

Her mum was about to reply, but she was interrupted by a little meeping cry from near her feet. She leant over to look into the carrycot she was rocking with one foot.

'Ahh, I knew he'd wake up with all the carry-on.' She waved at Emily. 'Can ye give him his bottle while I sort out Mrs Tumnus's sunburn?'

'Erm . . . yeah, sure,' said Emily, who wasn't. Facing down arch-villains was one thing, but holding the devil-baby was quite another.

She peered worriedly into the carrier, then—

'Woah, Mum, there's something in here!'

In the swaddling clothes and blankets was a little grey leveret, a baby hare. He had huge brown eyes, big front teeth and long black-tipped ears. Her mum frowned.

'Aye, precocious little beggar. He just changed when all the magic flooded out.' She frowned. 'I don't know what I'm supposed to tell the health visitor, sure.'

Emily eyed the little hare while she rummaged in the baby bag. How was it fair that he just changed like that? It had taken her years and she still hadn't cracked the horse. Stupid devil-hare-baby. She'd grabbed the milk bottle just as a herd of black horses with glowing red eyes came galloping down the street. They skidded to a halt outside and, with the *voosh* of a hovercraft, became a gang of Pooka led by a small white-haired old lady in a massive fur coat.

Maeve wouldn't let any of them but Mammy further than the front garden.

'Donal – I'm watching yeez, right? Keep yer light fingers to yerself. Mammy.' Maeve said, nodding to her ma. Things were still a little tense in that department.

'We came to see if we could help,' said Mammy, then, spotting the bottle Emily was still holding, smiled. 'Is that fer the wee fella?'

With that, nothing would do but that Mammy should see the baby. To Emily's great relief, she plucked both bottle then devil-hare-baby away, and stroked his long furry ears as she fed him. She nodded at Emily.

'Glad you got out in one piece, girl. We got swept out in the crowd. Came back with the clan to find yer trail and followed ye here.'

She turned to address them all.

'It's gone bad out there. That musical baggage has set the Hunt loose, and they're mad for Pooka blood.'

'Ah, that might have been something to do with Bron,' said Emily, and explained. Mammy grinned as she did.

'Ahh, her ma'd be proud, rest her soul. There's hope fer the girl yet.' Her smile faded as quickly as it had come. 'But none fer us if we don't get clear of the Hunt. If I can find ye, they can too.'

'Some hands came knocking already, and ye've just laid a big Pooka scent trail of yer own, right to my front door,' said Maeve, arms folded across her chest.

Mammy nodded. 'Aye, but we're riding straight on out of here once we've picked ye up.'

'We can't just abandon the wounded,' said Emily's dad.

Mammy's face was hard as she replied. 'I'm not suggesting as *ye* come along. Ye'd only slow us down.'

Alan looked as close to mortally offended as Emily had

ever seen him. Mammy's expression softened.

'Yer a fine man for a humin, but ye've only got two legs.'

'I can add two wheels to them and keep up, I believe,' he said, bristling.

Maeve touched his arm. 'Love, it makes more sense for ye to help Japonica get the wounded to better shelter,' she said. 'And take the little one too. We'll lead the Hunt away, and start to plan the fightback.'

Alan paused and considered for a moment, then nodded.

'You're absolutely right, you're better equipped for this.'

'Like always.' Maeve grinned. She passed him the baby bag. 'There's bottles. And a spare magic battleaxe.'

'I've been looking for that!'

'Mum, I'm coming as well,' said Emily from her seat at the bottom of the stairs. 'This is my fight too. Don't try and stop me.'

She gritted her teeth and braced herself for a public showdown.

'Of course ye're coming.'

'But . . . aren't you going to tell me not to go? I had a speech about wartime ready and everything.'

'No, this is too important.' Her mum shook her head. 'But this isn't a war. This is a disaster, and people need to be rescued.' She leant forward and kissed Emily's head, and the smell of paint and baby sick was a comfort. 'And ye're quite good at rescuing people.'

'I will be coming too, of course.'

They turned to see Tarkus, who was propped against the living-room door. It looked like it might be the only thing holding him up.

'Look, polis, no one's doubting yer courage,' said Mammy, 'but Donal can't be carrying ye again if he has to fight.'

Tarkus quirked an eyebrow.

'I don't think that will be necessary.'

He clicked his tongue, and up the front path trotted a white shining collection of ink marks that resolved themselves into a perfect horse.

'Painty!' said Emily. 'Where on earth did she come from?'

Tarkus shook his head, even as he grinned.

'I have absolutely no idea. I didn't even whistle.' He limped through them to press his head to Painty's – she was already nosing it through the door. 'Because you're a very clever horse, aren't you, yes you are.'

Maeve was eyeing Painty with a strange expression on her face. She reached out as if to run her hand along the long brush marks of her back, then stopped herself, and shook her head.

'Okay, everyone who's coming, ye've got ten minutes and we're out the door.' She glared around the hall. 'Emily, in the studio. I'd have words with ye.'

That seemed ominous.

Emily stepped into the crowded garage full of scrap metal her mum called the studio. Maeve thumped through the door not long after. She handed Emily a paper-wrapped package.

'Here, jam sarnies. Can't go facing the end of the world without supplies.'

'Never knowingly under-snacked.'

Their eyes met and they smiled. Her mum became serious again, as concentrated as Emily had ever seen her.

'Now, what else did I tell ye?'

'Erm . . . forgiveness is better than permission, but just legging it is easier?'

'No.'

'You'd be amazed at the good stuff just lying around in bins?'

'No, ye dafty! About the Hog.'

'Not to let him poo on the settee again?'

Her mum raised the narky eyebrow that usually preceded the gob.

'Oh, wait, never leave home without your hedgehog!'

'Exactly!'

Emily squinted at her. 'You also said he was just a normal hedgepig, so . . .'

'That I did. And so he is. But still. Keep him close.

He's . . . good luck.'

Maeve was doing weird stuff with her eyebrows as she spoke.

'Mum, if there's something you want to tell me about the Hog, now would be a really good time.'

Maeve looked like she'd bitten into something sour.

'I can't say, darl.'

'Oh, come on, it's the actual end of the world!'

Maeve's jaw muscles twitched and her lips pulled tight.

'No, I mean I literally magically can't say. I'm sworn to secrets and it's an oath that can't be broke.' She stood up suddenly. 'Tell me what the rule is again.'

'Never leave home without your hedgehog.'

'That'll be right.' And with that she walked out, shouting at everyone that they had five minutes. *Well, that was a weird conversation*, Emily thought. Even for her mum.

She came outside to find Tarkus leaning heavily on Painty, as the Pooka milled around them. He still looked dreadful.

'Tee, you don't have to come, you know. It's okay.'

He shook his head with the exaggerated care of a man with a serious headache. 'No, my place is here with you, until the bitter end.'

'Let's hope it's not bitter, eh?' she said, while trying and failing to smile.

'Indeed,' he said, but didn't look particularly convinced.

There was some kerfuffle behind them and Emily turned around, then groaned a terrible groan, and had to avert her eyes. Her mum and dad were kissing a far-too-passionate goodbye for old people.

'Man, today has already scarred me for life. This is too much.'

In all the commotion, darkness had fallen. From the distance, the bleak brassy peal of a hunting horn sounded, shrill and sharp. The Hunt were hungry for blood, and loose on the streets of modern London.

CHAPTER 18

Like a flock of goth crows, the Pooka clan gathered outside Emily's house. At their heart, three generations of Pooka women.

'There's no time left. We have to go,' said Mammy.

Maeve squeezed Emily's shoulder. 'If we're to do this, ye need to find yer horse.'

'Yeah, I know,' said Emily. '*So* glad everybody is watching.'

She looked inside herself where her other forms waited. The hare and hound hung there, furry and fleet. Beyond them the horse – all mane, flanks and muscular power, always beyond reach. But the hound and hare had been too, and she had mastered those. Why not again? She summoned up memories of the practice she'd done with her mum, of the hours of lessons and guidance from Mammy, of how to reach and find and just . . . be her other form. She gathered it all up, flexed whatever magical muscle it was she used, and tried with all her might to push further than she'd gone before.

It wasn't easy. At first, her whole being stretched and fought to grasp the horse, but it merely tickled her fingertips, like something out of reach at the back of a high shelf. But that tickle was all she needed to know it wasn't impossible, and once she'd realized that, she relaxed and it started to flow. Her new shape began to wrap over her – she didn't force it, just felt her way in. She usually had the dizzying sense of dropping as she shrank, but here she floated up as her eyeline lifted, and became steadier as her weight shifted on to four feet. Not feet, hooves!

Based on all her previous transformations, she'd figured she'd end up as a little Shetland pony, but she could see long, grey muscled legs. Craning her head, she could see another set at the rear. Good start, right number of legs and everything. With the swish of a black tail behind, she caught sight of her reflection in a car window. She didn't know what type of horse she was, but her coat was ruffled velvet over an athletic frame, and her neck was handsomely arched. She was sproingy, if sturdy. Like a racing sofa.

She shook herself, and a mane flicked and a tail swiped. The urge to run bubbled up in her, and she stamped her hooves and whinnied. Her mum and Mammy were both wearing wide pirate grins. Then, with a groan not unlike a time-travelling police box, two huge mares appeared, one black, one white, with three glaring red eyes between them. Emily bared her teeth and nickered, if that was the word. A ripple of horses appeared as the rest of the Pooka changed too. She could sense them all, sense her herd, and for a moment she felt like things might be okay.

The screech of the hunting horn sounded again, mere streets away now. There was another sound too, one much worse. A terrible roar, like a motorbike engine revved until it was about to explode. It reverberated off buildings and nearly caused Emily to have a horse-sized accident in the street that they'd have needed a shovel to clear up. It was the Bear. He was back with the Hunt and they were closing in. It was time to run. No, it was time to GALLOP!

And how they galloped. They poured through streets like a black tide, hooves scattering the glinting low-lying fog of spilt magic, red eyes flickering embers in the night. Mayhem caused by the collision of the two Londons was everywhere. Crashed pumpkin coaches, abandoned cars and roaming dragonets all mired the streets, but they didn't slow the Pooka for a moment. The flood of demon horses flowed over cars and around omnibuses and straight through an abandoned street party, tables, bunting and all.

As they ran, the sound of the Hunt drew closer. The horn blared louder and louder, accompanied by that paralysing roar of the Bear, and a distant metallic crashing as the Hunt smashed its way through obstacles the Pooka had flowed over. Despite the fear, Emily felt a hectic excitement building as she charged at full pelt. To be a horse was to be speed itself, her whole body aching to go as fast as she could for ever. A part of her horse self was quite looking forward to standing under a tree and eating a lot of lush grass at some point, but for now she was speed incarnate.

Her excitement was soon crushed by what she saw as they galloped. Most Daylight people were indoors now, hiding, twitching curtains at the terrors outside, but where they weren't, ugly scenes ensued. Night Folk and Day Folk clashing, equally terrified of each other. A blue-furred creature wolfing down biscuits while an elderly shopkeeper whacked it with a broom. Angry red-faced men shouting at cowering fairies who were flocking, confused, around a flickering lamp post. A tall green-faced woman in a pointy hat zapping a belligerent policeman into a toad with a purple flash of magic. Wait, had that been . . . ? Too late, they were past and still charging. No time to go back and help anyone, no time to do anything but run to beat the devil.

At some unseen signal, the Pooka clan began to split up. As they passed major junctions, little side streets, or gates into parks, Pooka would peel off. In ones or twos they galloped off from the main herd without looking back. Emily, unsure what to do, just stayed right on Mammy's tail. Soon it was just her, Mammy, Maeve and Tarkus on Painty. When Emily hurtled around a corner, she found Mammy and Maeve already transforming back into human form and waving for her to stop. She had to pull up sharply and found that it was possible for a horse to skid.

Emily changed back, then staggered as her feet touched the ground. Only two of them now, how was she supposed to stand up? She wobbled until her mum steadied her. Mammy handed her a package of cake, and she shovelled it in until the wooziness stopped.

'That is so much freakier than being a hare or hound.'

'Ah, it's always worse when ye've got a strong form, and that's a grand horse ye've got there.'

'Why have we stopped? Where has everybody else gone? We need to sort the Hunt out.' She spoke rapidly through the cake. 'I can't see them falling for the bridge again, but I think—'

'Darl, we've been chased by professionals for centuries. I reckon we can figure it out.' Her mum grinned, while Mammy raised a wry eyebrow.

'Oh,' said Emily.

'We talked,' said her mum, 'and it's ye who needs to figure this out, and ye'll not do it while running.'

'Whu—?' said Emily, helpfully.

'Look, ye've got that weird little brain that puts things together,' said her mum. 'Ye've done it time and again. I can't do that. I'm a fighter, not a thinker.'

'So we'll fight, while ye go an' think. Let them as can, do,' said Mammy, and crossed her arms quite decisively, which was a sign the discussion was over. 'The clan are laying a cross trail o' confusion so ye can get away.'

'But the Hunt. The Bear!' said Emily, her apparently weird little brain spinning. 'What will you do?'

'*Tch*. I've given that furry behind a right kicking once, a pleasure it will be to do it again so,' said Mammy with a curl of the lip.

'Oh, and keen I am to have words there too. The only person who puts my girl in mortal terror is me,' said Emily's mum, and held a fist up, knuckles white and angry. Looking at them both, Emily almost felt sorry for the Bear. Almost.

'So, we'll be fine, but not for long if this all isn't fixed. And I've watched ye, ye and the polis,' said Mammy, as she nodded at Tarkus. 'That's what ye do, ye fix things. So ye do that, and we'll do the breaking of things to keep ye safe while ye do.'

'I feel I should note, ma'am, that I'm not "polis" anymore, I'm afraid,' said Tarkus from the sideline.

'Fahh, you'll be a polis till you die,' scoffed Mammy.

'Uniform or no. It means looking after the city's people, and isn't that what ye're doing?'

'I – yes . . . I suppose so.' He gave her a surprised nod, and received an unexpectedly respectful incline of the head back.

'Now, get on with ye.' Mammy gave Emily a fierce hug and was already changing while Emily was still spluttering out bits of fur coat.

Her mum gave Painty another long strange look, and a very gentle stroke on the nose.

'Oh, here ye go.' Maeve rummaged in her jacket and handed Emily a packet of biscuits. 'Fer planning. Make one, then come find us. We'll be where yer dad and Japonica are moving the folk underground.'

'Okay,' said Emily in a small voice. The part of her that had recently been a herd animal was very concerned about all this. 'And my brain's not weird.'

'Ah, so it is. Ye're my daughter, aren't ye?' said her mum, giving her a squeeze. She spoke quietly in her ear then. 'It has to be ye. There's forces circling and ye're at the centre of it all.' She stepped back. 'So get yer weird on, darl.'

With the wheeze of an asthmatic balloon magician, she was a huge black mare again, galloping away, eyes flashing.

Then it was just Emily and Tarkus, Painty and Hoggins, alone in a time-wrecked London, with the weight of both worlds resting on their shoulders.

Tarkus covered their trail. He weaved the scents of the street together to disguise them both. He kept it up until they felt safe, then they tethered Painty in an alley and climbed a fire escape to the roof. They sat there now in the dark and silence. London, whose lights had been magnificent enough to stop Tarkus dead in his tracks a day ago, now flickered and fritzed. Half of the city was dark, and the other was only fitfully illuminated, a giant set of broken Christmas lights.

Above them, livid against the still orange-bleached dome of the night sky, were streams of darkness and hissing shadow. They writhed across the sky like giant jagged cracks, snaking down into a vast and glimmering black storm cloud that squatted over the centre of the city. It was the spilt raw magic of the Midnight Hour being pulled in, like rivers to the sea, by the Nocturne's cloak.

This was going to have to be a heck of a plan. It was going to require the list of all lists, the ultimate mind-map flow chart in different colour pencils, linking all the different pieces together, to figure out how to save the world. She was going to . . . really need a snack. Man, imminently world-ending disasters just made her *ravenous*.

Emily pulled out the jam sandwiches her mum had made, and the Hog came with them, caught chewing his way into the bag. She sat them on her palms, and weighed them both up. *Sandwiches. Hoggins.* Two of the best things in life. He grunted, scratched vigorously with a hind leg, and stared mournfully at the sandwich he'd been separated from. What had all that been about the Hog with her mum earlier? What was she 'sworn to secrets' about? He'd demonstrated some odd tendencies and she didn't think he was quite a normal hedgehog, but . . . she had no idea.

'So, as terrifying as it is that you are the person I have to ask,' said Tarkus, 'what is your plan to save the world?'

'You heard Cornelius. We just need to turn the Great Working off then on again, and it'll all be okay.'

'That's a goal, not a plan!' he snapped.

'It's good to have goals!' she protested, through a mouthful of jam sandwich.

'In self-improvement, perhaps! This is going to take more than wishful thinking, though.'

He'd started to pace and wave his arms around. Emily relaxed just a tiny little bit. Tarkus getting very annoyed was a key part of her planning process. She usually found it inspirational.

'Yes, the spell could, if restarted, put things back in their proper place—'

'I can feel a very negative "but" coming on,' said Emily.

'But . . .' he said.

'I knew it!'

'Cornelius was very clear.' He scowled. 'It requires an enormous quantity of magic, which *we do not have*, to start the clock and gather the rest of the magic in.'

'So if we had magic, we could get magic, but we don't have magic, and we need magic to get magic?' Emily scrunched her nose up while she thought about it.

Tarkus squinted as he worked that through, then nodded bitterly. 'Yes, and none of us have that magic, except for the Nocturne.'

He gestured at the rivers of captured magic flowing into the growing storm behind him. He slumped down on the roof next to her, and an acerbic twang of burnt garlic filled the air. 'So all is lost.'

Emily crossed her arms in a manner an outside observer would have said looked a lot like Mammy in a hard mood.

'No, I'm not having that. We've been in some proper rotten situations, most of which have been your fault,' she said, and continued talking before he could protest the gross injustice of this statement. 'And "all" has never been "lost" because I always fix it by coming up with a plan. I'm good at plans.'

Tarkus squinted at her. 'That is . . . faintly true, but there has been a large element of last-minute improvisation, whopping handfuls of luck, and I have been badly injured by a bear each time.'

'Exactly!' said Emily. 'Good at plans, like I said.' She

stood up and put her hands on her hips, now unconsciously channelling Maeve in a tanty.

'So come on, Inspector, don't go defeatist on me now.' She loomed over the gloomy ghûl. 'What are the options?'

'I don't know. I can feel the magic draining away already.' He sniffed the air. 'I don't know how we'd summon up vast occult forces.'

Emily paced around a bit, trying to pretend she was a consulting detective with a pipe, about to fire off some brilliant insights.

'What about the nightshades? They've got magic in 'em.'

'They're just a tiny charm.' He shook his head. 'You'd need hundreds of thousands of them to make it work.'

'Scratch that. Errm . . . could we make a bucket chain out of all the wizards and witch— I mean, sorcerously orientated ladies out there.' She mimed joining hands. 'Get everyone to put a bit in.'

'I . . . perhaps, but –' he held his hands up helplessly – 'even if it was possible, the Night Folk are in disarray across the city. How would we gather them in time for midnight?'

'Man, you're a negative Norman today.' She thunked herself on the head with frustration. 'There must be a way to get some spare magic from somewhere and— Hang on!'

She spun around, perilously close to the roof edge.

'Spare magic . . . different magic! What about the other sort – the nature sort, like the Antler Lady had got?'

'That is ancient magic.' Tarkus's eyes narrowed as he frowned. 'It is beyond and above even that of the Older Powers.'

'So it's perfect!'

Tarkus's whole face creased in thought, and he squeezed the brow of his nose.

'I just don't know. The Ancients do not dally with humans or folk anymore.'

'Antler Lady more than dallied! We had like a proper chat about stuff.' Emily was hopping with excitement. 'If we could find her again, I bet I could talk her into it. I'm extremely personable.' She heard Tarkus groan but ignored it. 'We just want to borrow some magic to get things working again.'

'It's not a cup of blood from next door!' he yelled. 'It's the primal force of the universe!'

'So she'll know where it is when she wants it back.' The arms crossed again. Connolly semaphore for a decision made. 'Come on, Flowers. We need to go and borrow some magic from a god.'

CHAPTER 19

'Right, come on then, Flowers, get your smell on.'

They were in a grotty play park in Herne Hill, scattered with litter. Tarkus had brought them here because it was one of the parts of London that used to be the Great North Wood. His people worshipped the Ancient Powers long ago as guardians of the land, and knew they could only be summoned somewhere that was or had been forest. Tarkus knelt on bouncy play park tarmac, amongst gusting crisp packets and the dwindling sooty mist of magic, with the expression of a man wondering how his life had come to this. He sighed a sigh so weighted with exasperation that you could almost hear it hit the floor.

'You're describing the most sacred rite of my people. Could you try to show even a modicum of respect?'

'Absolutely. Flower power – go!'

She heard him mutter something that sounded very rude, before he closed his eyes and extended his arms. He touched thumb and forefinger in the simple sacred gesture he often made, but now the rest of his fingers twisted around each other too. He brought his hands together and his fingers locked. He opened his eyes then and they roared with flames, dripping tears of liquid fire down his cheeks.

He opened his mouth wide, body tensed as if to scream, but nothing emerged except silence. Instead, the smell of the play park began to change. Where before had been the distant bin-stink of the city, now came something green and fragrant, the hint of thick pine, the perfume of gnarled oak, and leaves underfoot. Brambles, bluebells, and misty dawn. From him flooded a whole forest.

He'd changed the odour of things before. He'd made her smell of violets for days. He'd blasted the Bear with a stunning whammy of scents, but she'd never known him do something this vast and rich. It was sculptural, a forest in everything but physical form. At the edge of the park, Painty nickered with joyful surprise. Emily closed her eyes and it was as if she was far from the city, deep in the woods. She even thought she heard birdsong for a moment.

Wait, that was birdsong.

She opened her eyes and watched in wonder as a forest sprang into being. The glimmering white bark of birch and the rugged trunks of oaks filled the playground. The tired old swings, the streets and houses beyond, all merged into wood and leaf. The ground under her feet became wrinkled with mossed roots, and the crinkled bark of towering ash trees hemmed in behind her. It had been an autumn night, but now it was the early light of a fresh spring morning. The forest had returned.

'Whoa, Tee, I didn't know you could do this.'

Without stopping the intricate movement of his hands, he shook his head.

'I can't. This isn't all my magic.'

There was a rustle of leaves, the click of hooves on stone. The birds sang louder to announce her glory.

The Antler Lady had come.

She stood tall and straight, broad antlers jutting proud from her forehead. Her white fawn-spotted hair cascaded over her bark-brown skin, making the green of her moss gown all the more vivid. Glimpsed beneath that gown were the tips of black cloven hooves. Her eyes shone, the greenest things in the verdant forest. Her antlers dipped towards them.

'I accept your offering, ghûlama. You have brought the woods home to where they once were. I honour that.'

Tarkus bowed, but staggered as he did. He was hollow-cheeked and green. The sculpting must have taken a lot out of him.

'I am greatly honoured, my lady. I summoned them in your name, only to please you.'

He turned his bow into a perfect sweeping arm gesture that pointed to Emily. Smooth like a prince.

'There is one here who begs leave to speak to you.'

The Antler Lady's face lit up with a smile.

'Old friend, I knew I sensed your presence! Seceded or not, you need beg no leave,' said the Antler Lady in a husky warm voice. 'What do you wish of me, kinsman?'

'Erm, sorry, what?' said Emily.

The Antler Lady's smile vanished.

'I am talking to the hedgehog.'

The Hog had squirmed his way out of the satchel at Emily's feet. His little nose was all a-twitch. Grunting with excitement, he made a beeline for the Antler Lady before Emily could grab him. Fixing her with a beady eye, he began to circle her, crooning a constant grizzling noise. On every circuit he nudged against her cloven feet, before continuing his strange encirclement.

'Oh my actual god, what are you doing?' Emily gasped. 'I'm so sorry, he's never done this before.'

'This is the hedgehog carousel,' said the Antler Lady.

'The what now?'

'With his circling dance, song and occasional prickly nudges, he hopes to hypnotize me into an amorous state.'

'Amorous?'

'It is a courtship dance.'

'Wow. Just wow. He's drooled on your hooves, I'm so sorry.'

The Antler Lady gave a yipping bark, and the Hog stopped in his tracks.

'Not today, friend,' the Antler Lady said. She knelt and tickled him behind the ear spines and Emily could have sworn he purred. Emily seized her moment to scoop him up. She held him in her hand, his little legs still running in mid-air. This close to the Antler Lady, there was a different air, that of a cleaner and better time. It was like breathing in spring.

'*So* sorry about that. It's me who wants to talk to you though, your hornship.'

Tarkus groaned quietly behind her.

'Hmmm,' said the Antler Lady, and looked at her anew. 'That he chooses to travel with you speaks well of your character. What do you want?'

'Okay, big ask, but the spell that makes the Midnight Hour is broken and we need a lot of magic to start it again or everybody is going to die, and you've got the only magic left, because of the nature thing and, whoa, does that mean your magic is, like, organic?'

Why did her brain make her talk nonsense when she was nervous? *Why?*

The Antler Lady's solid green eyes glinted like emeralds, then she shrugged. 'These are the problems of the city. I am the forest.'

'But people are in trouble. People will die.'

'Everything dies if you wait long enough.' The silver velvet on her antlers glowed as she tipped her head. 'Then they turn to soil that grows more trees.'

'Lady, the ghûl are amongst those threatened.' Tarkus's eyes flamed with anger, but he spoke with great calm and precision. 'They are not of the city, but people of the soil who have always honoured you and your kind.'

She inclined her antlered head at him.

'True.'

'*And*,' Emily continued, 'the Hog would totally be really pleased about the whole thing. I'm a Hedgehog Friend too.' She pointed to the badge on her satchel strap. 'Fully paid-up member, see?'

Tarkus closed his eyes.

The Antler Lady looked at them, her face unreadable.

'Yes, it's city stuff, but cities are made up of people and animals and little bits of nature.' Emily was pleading now. 'London has so many trees it kind of is a forest. Please help us.'

The Antler Lady twisted her lip just a little.

'Your friendship to hedgehogs sways my view. Perhaps there is a case to be made.'

Never leave home without your hedgehog! Thanks, Mum.

'However, I cannot act unless an ancient law has been broken. That is our way and we must abide by it.' Her thick white eyebrows knotted as she thought. 'Perhaps this falls under the law of fealty? If those sworn to the Great Working have broken it, then I have liberty to act . . .'

Suddenly, her head whipped round so fast her antlers blurred. She gave a deep barking cough in her throat.

'*This* is what is wrong with your kind.' Her face was distorted by anger. 'All must eat, but killing purely for sport is against all laws.'

'Hang on, what?' said Emily.

Then the shriek of a long pealing brass note tore through the trees. Moments later, the huge form of the Bear smashed into the clearing. He was in his three-quarter form, thick with fur, his awful distended snout full of fangs. He reared up to his full height as he saw Emily and Tarkus.

'Cannot hide from Bear, flower boy. Not when making smells like this.' His great sensitive nose twitched violently. 'Wait, is that . . . ?'

He saw the looming antlered form glaring jade fire at him. To Emily's astonishment, he trembled, his fur shaking all over.

'Lady,' the Bear moaned, and threw himself to the floor, paws over his nose, eyes averted from her glory.

As he did, with a grating scritch and scratch, the pack of remaining hunting hands appeared, their nimble fingers clawing their way up trunks. Behind them came three vast, black, vicious-snouted wyrms, all that was left of the Hunt, glistening with slime as they slithered into the clearing. Atop them, gold-masked huntsmen armed with lances gleaming silver-sharp in the dawn light.

'What in Vlad Dracul's own name are you doing?' Peregrine Stabville-Chest's voice echoed from the golden helm in the middle. He flipped his visor open and his bone-white face peered out at the trembling Bear.

'Get up and murder them, won't you, there's a good chap.'

The Bear's only response was to move his huge killing paws up to cover his eyes, and start chanting in a thick guttural language under his breath. Peregrine sighed. He gestured languidly at the Antler Lady with his lance.

'Don't think whatever hedge-magic you've baffled his tiny mind with will work on me, you ghastly peasant.' He smiled, giving a glimpse of his shark-like dentistry. 'I'm a blooded peer of the realm.'

He kneed his wyrm further forward, and the hunting hands seethed around him.

'Now, get out of my way. This is Her Lady's Midnight

Hunt, and we shall claim our prey and put right a great injustice.'

He snarled at Emily, his fangs yellow-varnished bone spikes jutting out of a dead face.

'You would hunt in my eternal forest?'

The Antler Lady's voice was the bitter frost of a dark winter morning. She took a step towards the massive wyrm.

'You would hunt my kin for sport?'

Now her voice was an ice storm, enough to freeze sparrows to branches. Peregrine's wyrm slithered backwards, despite him digging his spurs in. He hesitated for just a moment, glancing at the Bear.

'You would kill for pleasure? You would take more than you need? You would break the ancient laws?' the Antler Lady said.

Peregrine looked around at the rest of the Hunt, and visibly steadied himself. He was in charge here. He definitely was.

'I am Lord Peregrine Stabville-Chest, of the revered, millennia-old vampiric line. Our family motto is *Omnes Bibendum*, literally "drink them all".' He smiled his terrible dead smile. 'We have been taking more than we need for ever, and I see no reason to stop now. And so ... enough of you.'

With that, he used his awful vampiric speed to thrust

forward with his lance. It shuddered in his arm as it hit, and he yelled 'Ha!' in satisfaction. Until his gaze followed the length of the lance to see the point resting in the Antler Lady's flat palm, where she had held up a hand to stop it. Her hand was unmarked. She closed it around the lance head and the metal crumpled.

'Ah,' said Peregrine.

All around them, the woods grew thicker and darker, while the Antler Lady grew taller and brighter, as if she'd pulled the dawn light into herself. Emily felt the ripple of tree roots stirring beneath her feet. The Bear was now back up on all four paws and sniffing the air frantically.

'Now, madam, I'm sure we can resolve this misunderstanding. My own mistress is a lady of great power and—'

Peregrine's anxious waffling was cut off by half a ton of bear hurtling past him to hurl himself through the closing gaps in the trees.

'The great beast knows what comes to those who break the ancient laws,' said the Antler Lady.

She was bigger now, not taller or wider, but filling more space, as if she was everywhere. She loomed vaster than the forest, because the forest was just a part of her. She was the woods and the world beyond.

The hunting hands stiffened as they were gripped by roots. They strained as brambles flowed over them, fingers and thumbs flickering an urgent sign language of despair.

In moments they had become nothing more than stumps and bumps in the forest floor. They twitched for a moment then were still.

'Everything dies if you wait long enough,' said the Antler Lady. 'You have waited far beyond your time, little dead man.'

Peregrine's face was twisted in fear now. He spurred his wyrm to flee, but it was too late. All three wyrms bucked and writhed but were stuck fast as the tide of forest overwhelmed them. They keened as the moss climbed their sides, greening them into stillness. Peregrine and the other two riders were trapped in their saddles. Their gleaming black-and-scarlet armour disappeared under the green flood.

'Madam, I beg you, please, have mercy,' gasped Peregrine.

'Oh, but I do,' said the Antler Lady, and her voice was great oaks breaking in a gale. 'All the dead become trees eventually. I spare you the wait.'

The light from her became that of the dawn sun breaking through a canopy of leaves. As the green light touched the three wyrm riders, they stiffened, dropping their lances as their arms lifted up to point at the sky. Buds sprouted from their fingertips, legs thickened into torsos to become the boles of trees. Leaves and tender twigs crept out of the eyeholes of the other two riders' masks. Emily took one look at Peregrine, whose golden mask was wide open as the change took place, then turned away.

Where the final members of the Hunt had been was now a rippling, moss-covered, root-riven bank, topped by three trees with strange twisted trunks. Glinting in the very top branches of each was a golden helmet.

'You killed them all,' said Emily, in a hollow voice.

'No, they were long dead. Now they are free.'

The Antler Lady was a normal size again now, but her face was gripped with a cold fury. 'These are the people you would ask me to save?'

'No, my lady, they—' said Tarkus, urgently, but she wasn't listening.

'Hunters, wreckers, takers of more than their share – like all of this world.'

Emily realized that she could see the park swings again. The forest was fading away.

'I will have none of this, nor will I act to preserve it.' The Antler Lady turned from them. 'Soon enough you'll all be gone, and the trees will return.'

'No, wait, please, you have to help us!' Emily begged her, but it was too late. The Antler Lady stepped between trees, the dawn light ebbed away, and the woods faded and became the night all around again.

She was gone, taking all hope with her.

CHAPTER 20

Emily stared around the dark and empty playground. The only sign that the Ancient Power had ever been there was a spray of primroses growing out of the spongey tarmac. Of the Hunt, there was no trace at all. There was no trace of her plan, either. Beside her, Tarkus slumped to his knees. He was pallid green and looked like he'd been wrung out.

'She had so much power. Just the smallest part of it and we could have saved everybody . . .' he whispered.

'I . . .' began Emily, then stopped. She didn't know what to say. That never happened. She slumped down beside Tarkus on the dirty floor, empty of all but despair. They stayed silent, thoughts full of what they'd just seen, and of what had been pulled from their grasp. After a little while, Painty ambled over to them, having somehow freed herself from where she'd been tied up. She inserted her big inkhorse head between them and nickered softly. Tarkus leant his head against hers and closed his eyes. Emily did the same, cradling the warm weight of the pocket hog in her hoodie.

There was no telling how long they might have stayed there if a voice like a rockslide hadn't rumbled from the darkness.

'Think night cannot get worse. Are wrong.'

It was the Bear.

He towered over them, huge and vile. He had escaped the Antler Lady's grasp, but not without cost. The green stain of moss covered him like mould. He'd been ripped ragged by vicious thorns but his claws were long, his teeth sharp, and there was murder in his eyes.

'Longest chase of Bear's life,' he snarled. 'Eat flower boy first. Already tasted Pooka today.'

Emily was on her feet in a flash, all fear burnt away by flaming anger.

'What do you mean, "tasted Pooka", you filthy old rug?!'

'Follow Pooka. Big fight. White wolf friend not lucky this time.' The Bear grinned a mouthful of knives. 'Magic run out. Without magic, wolf just old lady, but Bear still Bear.'

'Mammy, no!' screamed Emily. She reached for her hound form to attack him, but a hand grasped her wrist. It was Tarkus, still green, but grimly determined.

'No, he's mine.' He was swaying. 'It was always going to come down to this.'

The Bear grinned wider, delighted.

'Yes! Please try fight. Makes it better.'

'I choose not to,' said Tarkus. 'You are horridly furry and I am done with this.'

With that, his index finger and thumb touched, and he lifted his hand like a priest giving a blessing. The Bear growled, hefty paw raised for a killing swipe, then paused. His nose twitched and his ears flicked. The scent around them changed to the amber-scatter of autumn woods and fallen leaves. Surely Tarkus wasn't trying to summon the Antler Lady again?

Tarkus stood still, unbothered by the looming furry mountain of death. The Bear was still too, only his nose moving. Tarkus waved his hand and the scent changed again, to the shiver of snow, then the warm musk of the cosy den, and the embrace of the great winter sleep.

The Bear gave a colossal yawn. Inside the sculpture of fragrance, even Emily could feel how good it would be to curl up and sleep the winter away. The Bear plumped down on his haunches, and rolled on to his side, all murder plans forgotten. He curled up, and relaxed fully into his true bear shape. He covered his head with his huge paws, and began to snore.

'Woah, you used the smell force, Luke,' said Emily.

Tarkus nodded.

'I've always tried to fight him before, but we're not a fighting people.' He nodded at the snoring lump in Emily's hoodie. 'So, inspired by your spiky friend, I triggered his hibernation.'

He limped around the pile of Bear, like a builder examining his work.

'Perhaps Mother's right, and my talents do lie elsewhere? Mother . . .' he said, and his lip trembled. 'I pray they are okay.'

Emily squeezed his arm. 'We'll make them okay. I, *we*, just need to figure it out.' She hoicked a thumb at the ripsaw-snoring bear. 'What should we do about Goldilocks?'

Tarkus frowned. 'There's some very specific advice about what to do with sleeping bears – it involves letting them lie.'

Tarkus staggered then, and leant heavily on Painty to catch himself.

'Emily,' he said, in a half-strangled voice. He almost never used her name. 'If I get on Painty, can you lead her?'

He was painfully hauling himself on to Painty's translucent back.

'Of course, but why?'

'Because I think I've overdone it, and there's not enough magic to—'

Even as she watched, his eyes flickered and went out. He slid straight off Painty and hit the floor with a sickening thump. She shrieked and ran to him. He lay motionless, lips turning a horrid mossy colour. She felt for where pulses were supposed to be and something in his arm fluttered erratically off-tempo. She had no idea what a ghûl's pulse was supposed to be like, but that couldn't be good. His skin was cold. That definitely wasn't right; he normally radiated heat, like a compost heap.

'Damn it, Flowers. This is what you get for showing off!'

He grew paler, his face the white-green of light-starved plants. There was hardly even a wisp of the glittering magic fog left now. The magic really was draining away. His pulse slowed, and she felt a moment's relief, until it dropped from a disco beat to a funeral march. She had to press her cheek near his mouth to check if he was even still breathing. Up close there was a sharp tang of rotting leaves. Was . . . was he dying? There was no 999 for ghûls, no one she could ask for help.

'Don't die on me, Flowers, or your mum will kill me.'

He had saved her life so many times. This was her turn to save his, and she wasn't going to let him down. What could she do? She glared at the Bear. This was all his fault . . . so he could bloomin' well help fix it.

'I'd normally feel bad about this,' she said to the snoring Bear, 'but you are a horrible hairy git who has repeatedly tried to eat us, so you asked for it.'

She reached out with her Pooka luck sense. It was harder than usual with the magic leaking away everywhere. She redoubled her concentration and groped for the Bear's luck. It was coiled within him, a quicksilver roil of light. She grabbed hold and ripped out his glowing good luck, leaving only the darkness of ill-fortune behind. He muttered and growled in his sleep but did not wake.

His luck filled her to the brim. She was swollen with its silver flood. She pressed her hand on to Tarkus's chest and pushed the luck into him. She gave him all of it, jamming him full of good fortune, then sagged back, hollowed out by the energy passing through her. Tarkus didn't look any different. Her hand on his chest could barely feel a heartbeat. She'd given it her all, and he was still on the brink. Why hadn't the luck helped him? Was he too far gone? Tears ran down her cheeks and splashed on to her hands.

There was a crashing from the bushes around the edge of the playground. *Something big in there.* She summoned the last of her strength to grasp for her hound form. She would guard Tarkus with her life. Then came a *schloop* of displaced air rushing in to fill a space, like a suddenly blocked vacuum cleaner, and a figure stepped from the darkness.

'I've said it before, I'll say it again. A hard woman ye are t'find, so ye are.'

The shadowy figure resolved into a slim man who could at best be described as 'shifty-looking', wearing a battered old black tweed suit, red scarf, flat cap and a broad grin.

'Uncle Pat! You're alive!' Emily screamed, and threw herself into his open arms. She was enveloped in his scent cloud of tobacco cut with a sweet medicinal odour. She may have cried a bit, despite absolutely not being a crier.

'There there, niecelette,' he said, and awkwardly patted her shoulder.

'Pat, it's Tarkus, he's . . .'

He looked over her shoulder and winced. 'Here, let's have a look at yer man now.'

Pat knelt by the ailing ghûl, removed the red rose buttonhole from his own lapel, plucked the petals off, and popped them in Tarkus's mouth. He uncapped a small pewter flask from his pocket and tipped some of the liquid in along with the petals. He looked at the flask, shrugged and took a swig himself. There was a brief silent pause, then Tarkus sat bolt upright, eyes flaming like torches, shouted 'Hecate!', and flopped back down again.

Pat nodded with satisfaction. 'Just needs half a florist's and a nap now and he'll be grand, sure.'

Tarkus did look better. He was back to his usual teak colour and breathing normally.

'What was in that flask?' Emily said.

'Secret family recipe made from fruit and flowers,' Pat said. 'It's brought men back from the dead before.'

That was lucky. She sat by Tarkus, her hand on his shoulder.

'Oh Pat, where have you been? Mammy thought you were . . .' Her breath caught in her throat. 'Mammy . . . oh god, Pat, the Bear said that he'd . . . done something to Mammy. That she's . . .'

She couldn't say it. Pat shook his head, small smile never shifting.

'Mammy's fine. I'd smell it otherwise.' His nose wrinkled, and his eyes flickered red. 'They've tangled right enough, but, well, it'd take more than him.'

'Are you sure?'

'Sure enough to be sat with ye, not building a bonfire around him, so I am.'

'Oh, thank god.' Emily's stomach calmed. 'So, where have you been?!'

Pat extracted a small hand-rolled cigarette from mid-air, like the worst children's party magician ever.

'Well, there was a nasty thing with them Hunt fellas,

but I got away, then I heard one of me favourites was in fierce trouble and so off I went.'

'And here you are.' She smiled.

'No, not ye.' He lit the roll-up with a sulphurous-smelling match. 'You're a grand niecelette and all, but ye were fine.'

She glared at him. 'I was nearly eaten. Again.'

'Like I said, fine.'

'You have no idea how much therapy I'm going to need in later life. If I even have one,' she muttered, but he wasn't listening. He turned to shout over his shoulder.

'Are ye coming then?'

A figure emerged draped in shimmering night, with a pale face and long red hair (such great hair). It was Bron. She looked less Bron-y than normal though. Her proud head hung low, and her sneer had shrunk to a tight-lipped frown.

'Bronagh,' Emily said, and Bron flinched. Emily's mind boiled with a hundred vile things to say but the gob picked out the one true feeling inside her.

'Are you okay?'

Bron's eyes went wide, her lip quivered and, completely to Emily's surprise, she began to cry. Quietly first, then great wracking sobs that took her to her knees. Pat stood frozen. This was not his area. Emily knelt next to Bron and put an arm around her shoulders, the Midnight suit cool like lake water under her hand. Bron grabbed Emily and clung on for dear life. She sobbed and rocked, until eventually she was still, with just the sounds of sniffing coming from under the red mane. Emily gently let her go.

Bron gave a final loud and very snotty sniff, then tossed her hair back. Despite Bron's undoubted beauty, she was an ugly crier. Her pale skin was a blotchy wreck, her eyes pink and swollen. Emily remembered Bron wasn't that much older than her, despite all her posing and poise. Which also meant she'd lost her mum younger than Emily was now. Emily hadn't really thought about that before.

'I . . . I was wrong. She's not . . . It's my fault,' said Bron, staring at the floor.

A year ago, Emily would have jumped up, howled 'HA!', and done some kind of rump-shaking victory dance, but she wasn't there anymore. As it was, she mentally chalked up one million points to Team Emily, and said, 'Yeah, I reckon. So what are we going to do about it?'

Bron's head snapped up. 'We?'

'*We*,' said Emily. 'You helped break it, you can help fix it.'

Then, because she was a better person these days but not actually a total saint, 'If you can stand working with a half-breed daysie mongrel, that is.'

Bron flinched again, then, to her credit Emily thought, almost managed a grin. She gestured up with her chin. 'Looks like we're all daysies now, eh?' Bron rose to her feet in that graceful way she had, and stars gleamed in the folds of her suit.

She looked Emily straight in the eye.

'Ye'll never fix it. *She's* pulling all the magic that spilt out of the Hour into her cloak.' It was pretty obvious who the 'she' was. 'An' she's going to use the midnight chimes fer to bind it to her for ever.' Bron slumped. 'There's nothing we can do, she's too powerful.'

'Says the girl who punched her in the throat earlier.'

Bron looked up sharply. 'Ye were there?'

'Yeah. It was one of the bravest things I've ever seen,' said Emily. 'So I know between us we can work out how to fight her and fix things.'

'Ahh, what's all this talk of fighting?' said Pat. 'We're a constitutionally unreliable people. We don't fight, we sidle in a back door and wander out whistling with a pie.'

They both looked at him. His face was dreamy with the glory of misdeeds past.

'I remember one landlord loading a whole beer cellar on to a cart for me, just in time afore the pub inspectors got there.' He grinned. 'Who didn't actually exist.'

Emily coughed loudly to interrupt. 'Pat, I enjoy a TED talk as much as anybody, but do you have a point?'

He looked bemused. 'Gods no, 'tis just a grand story is all, sure.'

'Ooookay. Thank you.' Her gaze met Bron's in an

unexpected moment of mutual sympathy. 'I thought you were trying to inflict a learning moment for a second—' Lightning struck her brain then, and she was sure sparks were flying from her ears. 'Wait, hang on . . . loaded the cart himself . . . just before . . . using the midnight chimes . . .'

She hung in idea space for she didn't know how long and when she rejoined the real world, both Pat and Bron were staring at her, probably wondering if she needed medical help as well.

'Whoa. This could actually be a plan.' She shook her head as if there were wasps buzzing in it. 'But there's so many moving parts I can't make sense of it all.'

'And that is *exactly* why you're going to have to make a list,' said a weak voice from the floor.

'Tarkus!' squealed Emily. 'Are you okay?'

He smacked his lips and grimaced. 'I have the most appalling taste in my mouth. Like someone murdered an orchard.'

Pat nodded in satisfaction. 'Made from fruit, see?'

'You need to break it down into a list. I've seen you do it before,' said Tarkus.

'You're right.' She rubbed her sweaty palms together. 'Okay, no paper, so I'm going to have to do a head list in my mind pantry. Much shush needed.'

She closed her eyes and muttered under her breath.

'Mum, Dad, Japonica, Cornelius, Hunts-by-Night,

Jonesy, Mammy, Bron, Pat, Pooka, Night Post, Resistance, Hog!'

She repeated it again, like a mantra, then opened her eyes.

'Okay, I've got it. We need to go back. Right now.'

'But all you did was list our families and friends,' said Tarkus.

'I know,' she said. 'Who else do we ever need?'

CHAPTER 21

Emily's horse vanished as they neared Paddington Station.

The Pooka were all in horse form so they could travel faster, Tarkus clinging to Painty as they galloped. Emily's grip on that form weakened, and then it was gone, like having all your clothes ripped off by a great wind, leaving you spinning and starkers in the street. She gasped, stumbled, tried to steady herself with two legs she no longer had and fell flat on her face.

'Ow!'

With the whiffling sound of a big foam ball being hit by a bat, Pat jolted back into his human form too. He danced the extra speed off with a soft shoe shuffle though. Of all the Pooka powers Emily had inherited, grace was not one of them. Bron, still in horse form, cocked her long head on one side to stare at them.

'What just happened?' said Emily, hauling herself up.

'There's not enough magic here,' Pat said. 'I couldna change if I wanted to.'

He was right. Emily couldn't even feel her Pooka forms. There was barely a trace of the cindery fog of spilt magic. It was just like being in the real world, which of course, they were.

'Hang on, how's Bron still—'

She was interrupted by the sighing hiss of an off-the-boil kettle. Bron changed back, arms folded across her glittering chest.

'Because I wear Midnight,' she said.

'Bron, what *is* that suit?' said Emily.

'When my la— When *she* arrived here in a gale of escaped magic, she made a spell from tatters of Midnight to draw all that magic to her.' Bron picked at the star-dappled fabric, her lip curled with self-disgust. 'This is part of it, filled with magic enough to do her dirty work. She wears the rest herself.'

'I've seen it,' said Emily.

'It'll let her become something like a god if she fills it,' said Bron, face utterly absent of expression.

Nobody spoke.

Around them, in the tall canyon of glass and steel, something else was fading. There were no glitching ghosts of old London here, no phantom eel pie shop wailing from under an office block, no sign of the past at all. As the magic drained away, so did the remains of the Midnight Hour.

'We need to hurry,' said Emily.

Outside the great ripple of curved roofs that covered Paddington Station, three goats were gambolling amongst the bollards. Where there were goats, there was—

'Jonesy!' Emily shouted. The post troll arose from where he lurked behind the great white ironwork girders.

'Miss Emily!' He picked her up, grinning, and held her aloft before carefully placing her down. 'Me and a few of the boys are keeping watch up here.' Behind him now, she could see various other hefty forms.

'All else are down below, miss.'

'I've got a plan, Jonesy.' She squeezed his big hairy hand.

He nodded, face grim. 'Then I hope it's a good one, miss, as I don't see how we'll make it much further otherwise.'

They walked past him into the great curved shelter of the station, its immense roof arching over them in waves of glass and iron. Emily had never seen it so empty. The sweeping platforms and promenades were deserted, the flickering lettering of the display boards showed all trains as cancelled. Tarkus tethered Painty by a billboard showing a model lying on lush grass wearing mainly strategically positioned perfume bottles. Painty was already tucking into the grass as they headed for the ticket barriers to the Underground.

Before they went below, Emily looked across the platforms to the statue of the bear who had been named for the station. He had been inspired by the poor children who had been evacuated during the war. It was that war which had led them here. Japonica needed somewhere to keep the Night Folk out of harm's way. After hearing of the Blitz in the Hour, Emily's dad remembered that people had hidden in the underground train tunnels during the war, and suggested maybe they could again. Posties from the Resistance had spread the word all over London. Now, as they walked down frozen escalators deeper into the Underground, Emily was chilled by a sense of history repeating.

The station's platforms and tunnels were jammed full of Night Folk huddled together, wrapped in blankets and cloaks, clutching suitcases and treasured possessions. Families formed knots around their children and elderly. They linked clawed hands, pressed brows together, stroked fur and offered what solace they could. In the way of people who suffer such things, they were quiet. A small rustle of low-voiced conversation, some muffled sobs, but no wailing or raging. They sat mutely, normal lives ripped from them, and waited for somebody to tell them how to get them back.

Black-and-silver uniforms moved through the crowd with baskets of food and blankets, delivering aid where they had once delivered post. The Night Post, which had become the Resistance, was now the Rescue Service. Here and there, they held out nightshades over the most in need, to give them precious magic, but there were not enough to go around. Emily's pride flared at how her dad's colleagues, her friends, had stepped up to do something good and right during all this flood of bad and wrong. She would do the same, she promised herself, would make things right even if she had to die trying. The thought that she actually might die sent a cold shudder through her. If she couldn't make her plan work, more than her life was at risk. Everybody's was.

She was distracted from these thoughts by a storm of cursing in Irish. She grinned and followed the squall around a pillar to find Mammy: battered, torn, dripping blood, but very much alive and very much annoyed. Mammy sat on an upturned crate while Maeve hovered over her with a grimly determined expression and a big pad of bandages.

'If the blasted magic hadn't gone, torn the big furball into shreds I would have.'

'And if I'd got feathers and floated I'd be a duck,' said Emily's mum. 'Now fer the love of Danu, would ye just sit still an' be bandaged, woman?'

Mammy glared with suspicion while blood seeped from wounds in her chest.

'I dunt hold with all that modern quackery. Have you no got any good clean moss? And gin. Gin would help.'

Maeve sighed a martyr's sigh, and tried to fight past her to get the bandages on.

'I don't know why it is we're making such a fuss. Worse than this I had in the clan wars,' said Mammy. 'I lost—'

'An eye then, and it didn't even slow me down,' said Pat from behind Emily. 'Ye've mentioned it a time or three.'

Mammy and Maeve both jolted, and a huge grin flashed across their faces, before it was replaced with fierceness. Within moments, they were both belabouring him for having the sheer cheek to not be dead, and didn't he know how to send a messenger bat, and to be sure it was a poor showing even with the list of terrible disappointments he'd visited upon the clan before. Mammy walloped him with a rolled-up newspaper, which Pat said just showed how pleased she was to see him.

Emily's dad ran over to join them, sword and battleaxe at belt, papoose with devil-hare-baby on back, and Emily was swept into a fierce wordless hug by both of her parents.

'Too tight! Too much fuzzling,' she squealed, but she felt warmed down to her toes by it.

Mammy's nose twitched, and she looked up sharply. 'Ye might as well come around, Bronagh. It's not like I can't smell ye're there.'

Bron had hung back behind the pillar. Now she haltingly joined them, head down and hair covering her face, a scared child awaiting punishment. Emily stepped right up by her.

'She knows that she was wrong, Mammy, and she—'

Mammy turned her single glowing red eye on to Emily and she shut up.

'This is clan business, girl. I decide how it goes.'

She turned that piercing gaze on Bron now. Even battered and bloody, Mammy managed to make the old crate she sat on look like a throne. Bron trembled but raised her head to meet the gaze. Nothing was said for a long while, then Mammy reached out a bloodied hand to her.

'I held this out to ye once, and ye turned away,' she said, her face hard as iron. 'I hold it out again now fer the love I bore yer mother, and that I still bear for ye.'

Bron stared at it, unbelieving. 'But I've done such—'

'We've all done things. Families forgive.' Mammy's eye flashed scarlet. 'Don't turn away again though, Bronagh, fer it's the last time I'll hold out my hand.'

Bron knelt before Mammy, and pressed her lips to the back of her hand. Once she had, Mammy gently tucked a thick strand of Bron's red hair back behind her ear, away from the silent tears that ran down her cheeks.

'We'll work it out, girl. Never fear.'

Later, Emily walked to the front of the little crowd that had assembled together in a storage space they'd found amongst the Underground tunnels. Posties, Pooka, parents, Poswa of the polis, and even some people who didn't begin with P. Tarkus was at the front, and seated on each of his knees was a long-haired bundle with glowing eyes. His sisters, brought here by Hunts-by-Night. Next to him sat his mother, force-feeding him deep-fried petal treats. He traded long-suffering eyebrow raises with Emily. *Parents, whatchagonnado?* Emily's mum and dad, Mammy and Pat and Japonica were sat next to them, and spread out behind them were all of the assembled faces of the family, friends and allies she'd found along the way.

These were people now prepared to listen to her, because she'd proved herself again and again. And also, she tried not to think, because no one else had got the faintest clue what to do to save the world. This was a deep-breath moment if ever there was one. She didn't take one though, just started talking before she quite knew what she was going to say. It usually worked.

'So, I normally have a flash of inspirational genius at this point and I'm not saying I haven't but the flash was that I'm not good enough for this.'

She held a hand up to forestall the objections. She imagined she'd heard some. Definitely.

'I mean, I'm not doubting my own genius, but I can't fix giant clocks, or fly, or do ninja stuff, or any of that.'

She pointed at her audience.

'But I have friends who can, so we have to get the whole gang together to fix this.' Emily hiked a thumb at herself. 'I'll still be doing a vital part of the plan though, because there is one thing I'm very good at – I'm extremely annoying.'

There were definitely no objections this time. Her mum actually nodded.

'Hrrrm. So then, it's a last-minute plan, but not the actual *last* last minute, which is the really clever bit . . .' She trailed off as people began to look confused. 'I'll explain that later, but first, somebody else is joining the team.'

She gave a whistle and Bron stepped forward from where she'd been staying out of the way. There was a hiss and a rumble from those who recognized her as the Nocturne's right-hand woman. A ripple of anguish passed over Bron's face.

'Somebody I trust,' Emily said as Bron looked at her with surprise. 'Somebody who is family.'

Emily unclipped a chain around her neck and handed Bron the whole necklace of bad pennies.

'Here, I want you to hang on to these. You'll need them.'

Bron went white. Well, whiter, anyway.

'But why?' Bron whispered.

'Because you're going to help fix it, right?'

Bron nodded and her hands closed on the necklace. She stood a little straighter.

'Anyway, it's kind of a swapsies deal, but I'll tell you about that in a minute.' Emily gestured to a heavyset tweed-clad figure in the crowd. 'Cornelius, I need you to answer some very important questions. Keep the fish analogies to an absolute minimum, yeah?'

It would have taken hours, but they didn't have hours. The magic had run out, and midnight loomed ever closer. So they squeezed all the hair-pulling frustration, serious parental objections, one tantrum (Mammy), and a near-walkout (Cornelius) into the time they had. After it all, when Emily's brain was so squiggled by thinking and people and timings that it felt like a squashed cheesecake, they had something that was almost a plan. And 'almost' would have to do, because they had to go. Missions were assigned, clothes were swapped, post bikes were oiled, and prayers were said.

People were rushing around everywhere but Emily found herself without anything more to do until her deeply worrying big moment later. She sat on the edge of one of the platforms, dangling her legs over in a way that would normally be inadvisably illegal. She sat in silence and watched the moving fairy lights of sprite larvae play in the dark of the tunnel beyond. A smell of warm rosemary bloomed and Tarkus sat down next to her.

'Well, it's so ridiculously unlikely that it just might work, right?' said Emily.

'What does that even mean?' said Tarkus.

'It's like what they say on the telly. "This plan's so crazy it just might work."' She added an American accent to be more convincing. His expression suggested she wasn't.

'You've spoken of this tell-you box before.' He gave her his patent narrow-eyed stare of doubt. 'You said it was full of lies and masquerades.'

'Well, yeah, that too. Bad example.' She gave him a long look. 'Are you okay?'

He just raised his hands and gestured wildly at . . . everything.

'Yeah, fair enough,' she said. They sat quietly together for a while.

'Thanks for saving us from the Bear,' she said. 'Again.'

He nodded politely. 'Last time though,' he said. 'I'm not doing bears anymore. They're so last season. I'm thinking dragons next. Possibly basilisks.'

They smiled at each other. Thin-lipped small smiles that didn't pretend they weren't both scared. The air around them filled with scents of sage and honeysuckle. He stood, and squeezed her shoulder. Just once.

'You need to get changed. I'll see you before I leave.'

He walked away, leaving her alone.

She reached into her hoodie pocket, ferreted around a bit and extracted the Hog. He looked at her. He seemed kind of sad, but it was always hard to tell.

'One last adventure, buddy.'

He scratched at what she really hoped wasn't a flea. She held him up closer and studied him. The ripple of his spines as he moved, the colour change from white at the sharp tips to ivory then dark brown at the base. The brownness of his nose tapering to black at the end. His dark dark eyes.

'Hog, if you were more than just probably magical, now would be a really good time to show it.'

He closed his eyes and tucked his legs in, his classic 'totally going to have a little snooze' position.

She rocked her hand to wake him up.

'Come on, don't make me stage a hogtervention here.'

At that, he just rolled into a ball.

She shook her head and eased him back into her pocket.

'Ow, spiky!'

CHAPTER 22

Emily's magnificent plan ran into problems before she'd even got to Parliament Square. The streets were cordoned off by the gun-toting police officers and soldiers from earlier, now glassy-eyed and patrolling the area in jerky dance steps, their heads tilted as they listened to the mosquito whine of the Nocturne's musical spell of control. There were more than ever before, as if waves of reinforcements had been marched in, only to fall under the Nocturne's influence too and join the tranced dance.

All the Pooka (apart from Bron, who was off up to secret stuff) had come with Emily to keep her safe. They'd tried to leave Mammy behind babysitting because of her injuries, but that hadn't gone well. Now, the devil-hare-baby was with Tarkus's mum back at Paddington, while Mammy and Maeve marshalled the Pooka to deal with the heavily armed occasionally breakdancing threat ahead. The Pooka were unfussed by it. They'd been avoiding the forces of law and order their whole lives. Precious night-shades were popped open, some of the only reserves of magic in the whole city, and luck was pushed. The patrolling forces all somehow looked the wrong way or did the robot, just as the Pooka silently glided through their lines.

But all of their luck ran out as they rounded the corner into the square.

'Errr . . . I don't remember yer mentioning an army o' dead fellas,' said Pat. Above the square, above all of London now, hung the Nocturne's Midnight cloak. Threads of smoky magic still poured into it from every part of the sky, but they were thinning out now, rivulets instead of rivers. Nearly all of the magic that had spilt from the Midnight Hour had been sucked into it. It was so vast and bloated that it had billowed out to look like a boiling cloud system, with a tornado-sized tail stretching back down to the square that dwarfed the tower of Big Ben behind it. In the centre of that glittering twister of magic and Midnight, far from the ground, hung the Nocturne, the queen of air and darkness, eyes shining lightning blue. Her ethereal background music echoed around the square. The Pookas' more immediate problem, though, was far below her. A great circle of the Dead were gathered around this storm of magic.

'There really are a lot of yer men, sure,' muttered her mum.

The Dead. The elite one per cent who worshipped the myth of an empire of the night, upon which the sun would never rise. Who'd helped make this whole disaster happen in the first place. The ground near the twister tail was covered in sooty fog – raw magic still being reeled in by the unstoppable force of the Midnight cloak. The Dead, desperate for magic to sustain them, were thronged around it, drawn to its anti-light like goth moths.

The vampires, the Hungry Dead, were top dogs, having been dead longest, and they hogged the centre, basking in the magic. Around them, in circles of social importance, were first the mummies – the Walking Dead – jade glinting from their dusty bandages. Behind them floated the ghosts – the Restless Dead – flickering through their final agonies, or glowing louchely in velvet pantaloons, depending. The light they cast lit up the ravaged rotting flesh of the zombies – the Shambling Dead – who formed the outer edge of the crowd. Around that edge sped a chugging hissing clanking contraption. It was the Postmaster in his steam-chair, who Emily decided probably represented the Deeply Annoying Dead.

Emily was looking at her watch with concern.

'We don't have time for this.'

'Well, I guess we'll just have to hack our way through,' said her mum. She didn't look entirely displeased by the idea. Nor, after what they'd suffered under the Hunt, did the rest of the clan.

'No, hang on,' said Emily, whose brain was fizzing again. 'I reckon I can fix this without fighting.'

'How sure are ye? If ye're wrong, they'll eat ye alive.' Mammy gave her the (one) evil eye. 'Not. A. Mettyfer.'

'Trust me.' Emily nodded at the Dead and the Older Power hovering over them like a malevolent Christmas tree fairy. 'Someone just needs to tell these guys the facts of Death.'

As she came out from hiding, she wished that Tarkus was with her, but his part of the plan had taken him elsewhere, somewhere he was really going to hate getting to. Oddly, this cheered her up.

She walked out behind the crowd of Dead, took a very deep breath, then . . .

'OY! Addams family reunion! A word.'

She'd used full gob volume. Her voice cut across the square like a motorbike in a church.

A thousand pairs of eyes, rotting, red, glowing and all

Dead, turned to stare at her, and a thousand mouths opened in hunger. There was a shrill squeal of compressed steam, and the Postmaster roared into view. He screeched to a halt, dried-up body rocking in its restraints, his severed hand hopping up and down like an angry white spider.

'You! I know you!' he roared through his speaking horn. 'Filthy criminal daysie scum!'

Emily folded her arms across her chest. 'Nice to see you too, mouse brain.'

A small mouse popped its nose out through the Postmaster's empty eye socket then disappeared back inside his cosy head.

'Lord Stabville-Chest was hunting you down. Where is he?'

Emily smirked. 'Peregrine? Oh wow, yeah, bad news on that front. He's, like, a shrubbery now.'

The chair nearly did a wheelie. 'A *shrubbery*?! You will pay—'

'Yeah yeah, grim death-related threats. Heard it all before.' She raised her voice again, talking over the Postmaster to the vengeful crowd behind him. 'I'm here to ask all of you one question!'

Every gaze burnt into her.

'What makes you think the Nocturne's going to give you any magic?'

'What?' The mosaic of faces shifted and changed as the

Dead looked at each other.

'You heard me. She's got nearly all of it. When's she going to give you any?'

She pointed up, where the mistress of them all hadn't even bothered to look down at the commotion.

A big blond vampire, bloated like a blood-drunk leech squeezed into a white frilled shirt, spoke up. 'Well, once it's all sorted out of course. At midnight, I imagine.'

There was a chorus of nods and noises of assent. Of course.

'Oh, right,' said Emily, 'because from what I can see you're standing here starving while she's at an all-you-can-eat mystical buffet up there.'

'Nayyysayer!' the Postmaster howled through his speaking horn. 'All of this will be sorted out by our betters, then we'll be great again!'

'Mate,' said Emily, almost with sympathy. 'You're having to stand in her dust to survive.'

'It has to get worse before it can get better,' he shrieked.

'Yeah? Look at these guys.' She pointed at the zombies. 'Look at Crumbledore here. He's on his way out.'

The zombies were going to pieces in the crisis. Literally. Pushed to the back, just outside of the fog of sooty magic particles, they were starting to disintegrate. Fingers, noses and toes were dropping off all over. As the cloud of remaining magic was pulled further in towards the centre, it was getting worse. There was the thump of a badly stitched-on arm falling to the ground even as Emily shouted.

'Why don't you ask her, you muppets? I bet no one has.' She shook her head in weary disgust.

'If you want something done . . .' Emily muttered, then dancing past the Postmaster she yanked his speaking horn off the steam-chair. As he squawked in (much quieter) outrage, she used it to megaphone-yell into the storm above her. 'Oy, Tinker Bell! What do this lot get?'

There wasn't even a flicker of response from the floating Nocturne.

'What's your brave new world going to be? Who gets all the magic?!'

Still nothing, but the crowd, urgently whispering, began to subtly, then not so subtly, push to get closer to the centre. Even the Postmaster was edging his chair inwards. She'd nearly got them.

'Come on, wake up, sheeple! She's actually pulling the magic out of you.'

Luminescent blobs of light were beading, wobbling, then shedding from the ghosts. The light dripped like gravity-defying candle wax, straight up into the storm above. That did it. They began to shriek. They called up at the Nocturne, yelled for answers, shook fists and talons. They were the very best of society and they demanded their share.

This noise did reach her, and her glowing sapphire gaze swept the crowd. She inclined a hand and floated down through the twister tail of the storm the Midnight cloak had become, until she hovered only ten feet above the crowd. Her face and hands gleaming white from inside the whirling darkness. Silence fell again, broken only by the eerie strains of her music. Immortal killers looked down at their dress shoes, renders of flesh and haunters of houses shuffled where they stood like naughty schoolchildren. No one was prepared to speak up.

'Oh for the love of . . .' said Emily, and looked up to meet the radioactive glow of the gaze that bored into her.

'Ask her,' Emily said, the silence so complete she no longer needed the speaking horn. 'She never lies. She just doesn't tell the whole truth.'

The big blond vampire who had spoken earlier was shoved forward. He shot a filthy look behind him, then cleared his throat.

'Erm, my lady, Great Lady, when exactly do you think you'll have enough magic to give us our share?' His fingers fiddled with the white flounces of his dress shirt. 'I imagine we'll all get a cloak, yes?'

The Nocturne spun in mid-air to turn her gaze to him, and he looked away from the light of her eyes.

'There will be no sharing. No cloaks.' Her voice was sweet and melodic, the heavenly gust of music underneath making her words seem perfectly reasonable until you actually listened to what she was saying.

'Ahh, righto, yes, jolly good, but obviously you'll be making this world eternally dark as promised?' said the barrel-chested vampire.

'I made no promises beyond breaking the Hour and bringing magic back into the Daylight world.' Her eyes were lasers now. 'I swore no oaths as to afterward.'

'Man,' said Emily. 'Have none of you learnt to read the small print in the last two hundred years?'

The vampire's eyes bulged, and there was a great rustling from the crowd around him. 'But – but – we were to rule again. The empire of the night—'

'Is no concern of mine,' said the Nocturne.

There was a sound like a gust of wind as the whole crowd gasped in horror. The Nocturne rotated in place above them, face not even cruel, just simply untouched by their plight in any way. Emily wasn't sure who spoke first, but it started as a whisper, grew and was repeated until it became a roar.

'Give it back! Give! It! Back!'

The whole crowd surged towards the central column of magic in which the Nocturne floated, every Dead voice and unbeating heart now full of righteous rage. They screamed and clawed up at her, fangs exposed, eyes desperate.

'Give it back! Give it back!'

In moments they had gone from cringing to a riot. The vampires were the vanguard, a mass of sharp talons and yellow-stained fangs clawing up towards the Nocturne. Hopping on the shoulders of others and pushing up from the ground in a pyramid of teeth and vengeance. The ghosts were not chained to the earth, and furious spectres dive-bombed the Nocturne while mummies and zombies hurled their wrenched-off limbs at her. The Nocturne vanished under the vicious swarm.

Then the music changed. The Nocturne's ever-present background music became a needle-like whine of violins sawing at speed, enough to make Emily wince. The world flickered around her, the sooty particles of magic in the air sprang towards the tornado tail of the cloak. The column of magic pulsed, then bulged and warped, like a giant golf ball passing through a hosepipe. In moments the air was completely clear. A deep lurch shook Emily from within as the fog vanished. The Nocturne had used the cloak to vacuum all remaining magic out of this whole area. Not a scrap of magic was left in it at all.

This posed a problem for the Dead. They were powerful beings beyond the laws of normal nature, but they were walking (sometimes floating) corpses and phantoms sustained only by magic. Without that magic they were just ... dead.

And so, the Dead ceased to be. The magic that held them in this world was ripped away and they crumbled back to what they would have been by now – dust. Just dust. The crowd collapsed in on itself in whooshes of thick white powder. The ghosts lost their shape and became light that drifted away on the breeze. The vampires simply burst and their clothes fluttered to the ground. All that was left were piles of dried-up bandages, rotting rags and oddly neat stacks of formal evening wear and velvet ballgowns. Dotted all around were black silk top hats, resting neatly on top of the piles. In the middle was a steam-powered wheelchair, which contained nothing more than dust, cobwebs, and some very confused mice.

The Nocturne descended, spiralling down from the storm cloud of her power above, lightning in a killer blue dress. A dread roll of deep bass notes made the ground throb underfoot as she gently touched the earth. She smiled at Emily, blue eyes aglow like the heart of a nuclear reactor. A shark's smile, all teeth, dead eyes, and hunger.

'If I would destroy a thousand of my own, child, what do you think I'm going to do to you?'

CHAPTER 23

The Nocturne stood before Emily, apocalypse eyes aflame. She was more than just her normal terrifying self, she was power incarnate. Her music throbbed around them, thick as fog, and the Midnight cloak filled the whole sky, a shadow spilling out from her. Her smile was the worst thing of all. Delighted. Hungry.

Emily's legs filled with ice and she couldn't move or speak. She was even struggling to breathe. Facing the Dead had been one thing, but this was too much. This was how Tarkus must be feeling on his mission right now, facing the thing he was most scared of in the world – heights. She wasn't going to be able to do it. Everyone was going to die.

Then a hand was placed on each of her shoulders. Her mum and Mammy, grim-faced but rock-steady. Behind them Pat, Donal and the rest of the clan. The Nocturne sneered.

'The whole filthy litter.'

Her voice was normal, yet as big as the sky.

'Call my little girl filthy and flatten ye I will, ya wagon,' said Maeve, chin stuck out pugnaciously.

'Mum,' hissed Emily. 'I'm not little anymore.'

Her mum ruffled her hair. 'Ahh, ye'll always be little to me.'

'Ye sure about this?' Mammy whispered.

'Abso-blooming-lutely not,' Emily said. She looked down at her watch as she spoke. 'But it has to be me, and it has to be now.'

Her family had her back. Her other family, those bonded through friendship, were off trying to fix things right now, and her only job here was to protect them so they could do it. That was enough to melt the ice that filled her. She didn't dare look at Mammy or her mum again; she just stepped forward instead before she could change her mind.

She walked towards the Nocturne, which felt about as sensible as approaching a ticking atom bomb or a deeply aggrieved T-rex. Her hair uncurled and stuck out as static prickled over her. It was the sheer concentrated force of magical power coming from the cloak. Where the Nocturne had stepped out of the pillar of shifting darkness to menace Emily, the original cloak could be seen, draped around her shoulders, clasped at her neck by a glowing star, and reeling out behind her to connect to the vaster part lashing back and forth above them.

Emily stole a glance at Big Ben, undamaged in this world. The small silhouette of a flying bike and its riders stood out against the illuminated clock face. The huge hands behind them pointed to 11.41 p.m. Nearly time for the end of the world. She knew it would end much sooner if the Nocturne happened to look up as well, so she carefully angled her walk of doom off to the side, forcing the Older Power to look away from the clock, and straight at her.

This was regrettable, because there was no place on earth Emily would less like to have been than in front of those eyes. As ever, fear made her sarky.

'Something's different about you, I can't quite figure it out. Is it your hair?'

The Nocturne smiled, but Emily was certain it wasn't because she'd found it funny.

'So in love with humour. Thinking words matter, that there is nothing you cannot talk your way out of.' The blue eyes flashed. 'And here we are again, child. I could indulge you while I have time to kill –' Emily really didn't like the way she pronounced 'kill' with such relish – 'or instead just destroy you and your entire family now, before you enact whatever your pathetic little plan is.'

She ran a long white finger over her chin, as she mused.

'Which would you choose in my place?'

'Oh, like you'd miss the chance to tell us all how brilliant you are.' Emily tried to sound calm despite the chill that flooded her. 'If music needs one thing, it's an audience.'

'There's some truth to that, child.' The Nocturne actually laughed. It was a sound akin to breaking glass and children shrieking. 'I did say I'd only kill you after I'd destroyed everything. You gain a small respite.'

Her face was hard as stone in an instant.

'But that only applies to you.'

She snapped her fingers and a wave of music, the screech of a thousand radios, vibrated behind Emily and crashed into the assembled Pooka. It toppled them like skittles, and they thrashed and shouted on the floor, clutching their ears. Even the edges of the sound were enough to make Emily stagger as she screamed.

'No! What are you doing?'

The Nocturne's smile was genuine, and dreadful beyond measure.

'I like an audience, you're right, but I love a show too.' The Nocturne's eyes were dead pools of light above her smile.

The fallen Pooka twitched and moaned, drowning in the unbearable noise. Emily had to force herself to look back at the Nocturne. She had to hold her attention. Over the Nocturne's shoulder, she thought she could see an all-too-familiar figure dangling from the ledge below the clock face. Was it Tarkus? Had he fallen? Where were the others? She . . . she couldn't help. She could only play her part, and trust the plan. She made herself look the Nocturne in her eyes.

'Forget them, it's me you need to worry about.' She tried to force her usual cocky tone out, but it sounded hollow even to her. 'How many times have you thought you'd won, and I've ruined you, eh?'

The Nocturne frowned.

'Hmmm . . . bored now,' she said, her porcelain cheeks tinted a cold blue by her throbbing eyes. 'This is less amusing than I'd hoped it might be. Now I have become so power-ful, you are merely an insignificance.'

And with that, she started to turn back to Big Ben, pausing only to smile at the writhing pile of tortured Pooka.

No! She couldn't! This called for a heroic effort, and the only superpower Emily had was knowing exactly the right words to drive someone to fury. She let the gob loose.

'I'm not here to ruin you!' she shouted. 'I'm here because I feel sorry for you. I want to help.'

The Nocturne stiffened, and stopped. Sometimes the words didn't even need to be rude.

Even as her family shivered in agony behind her, and her best friend dangled over certain death, Emily fought to keep her voice calm and her eyes on the Nocturne.

'Your sister told me you used to be kind, when you were the Madrigal.'

The Nocturne's whole body shuddered at this mention of her forgotten past.

'To be left alone like that in the Black Death –' Emily spoke quickly now, every word a sharpened dagger – 'to starve out of existence with no music to feed on . . . it must have been terrifying.'

The Nocturne swung back around now, her eyes flaming with light. Above them, the fabric of the whole cloak-covered sky was wracked by sudden winds.

'*Enough!*'

The noise was so great that something inside Emily's ear gave way. She clutched at it as warm blood trickled down her neck. The Nocturne was wrapped in a nimbus of shadow and lightning, her face wild with anger.

The gob had struck again. The worst part was that as Emily had been speaking, she knew it all to be true. She did feel sorry for the Nocturne. Although she mainly felt sorry for herself now. Would she even survive the next few minutes?

'You dare presume to know my heart? To pity me?!'

The static electricity in the air rose to such a pitch that Emily's hair wasn't just crackling, but smouldering. The Nocturne was floating now, her feet drifting off the ground as the cloak's power washed through her.

'Our dance is over. You die now.'

Emily gulped. 'Hang on, I thought you weren't going to kill me until last?'

The Nocturne's smile split further across her face than a human's could. 'You changed my mind.'

'Ah,' said Emily. She might have overdone it a bit.

The Nocturne floated towards her, the cloud of the Midnight cloak swirling behind. Her hands sparked with the same sapphire light that filled her eyes, power arcing between them, power like she'd never had before, the lethal strength of raw magic.

Emily half-closed her eyes, waiting for an awful zap, then . . .

Saved by the bells.

The unmistakable sound of the quarter bells.

The first lilting notes of their chimes tumbled out into the night air of London, as they'd done nearly every night since 1859, chiming their century-old sing-song ditty.

All through this hour, Lord be my guide; That by thy power, No foot shall slide.

The Nocturne whipped around to stare at the clock.

Emily looked up too, and there was no sign of a dangling ghûl.

'So quickly, but how . . . ? Oh, you ridiculous child.' The Nocturne laughed out loud. 'Did you think that would fool me?'

Emily tensed up all over.

'Did you honestly hope to make me angry enough to distract me from midnight?'

The Nocturne floated above her, shoulders shaking with laughter.

'When I have everything I've ever wanted within my grasp? Pathetic.'

Silence fell – the pregnant gap before the main bell struck midnight. The Nocturne turned to the clock.

Then turned back.

'Oh, I nearly forgot.'

As Big Ben chimed out the first bong of midnight, the Nocturne released the great bolt of pure magic energy still sparking in her hands, and shot Emily straight in the heart.

Emily thumped to the floor, her eyes flickering, legs twitching as the cold death magic burnt in. Blackness crept over her sight, and the last thing she heard was the sound of Big Ben tolling out midnight and the end of the world.

With the wreckage of her enemies and their dreams scattered around her, the Nocturne held her hands out in a conductor's pose. She made one small gesture and the bloated boiling mass of magic that covered the sky was at her command. It swirled and rippled and moved as one towards the clock tower. Sparkling with the galaxy of power within, it drowned the tower in black velvet, making it invisible against the night. The most magical artefact on earth wrapped in all the magic left in the world. From within its darkness came the faint glimmerings of an emerald light. It grew and grew, the very tower of the clock lighting up with sorcerous energy as it drew in the enormous mass of magic that had been placed upon it.

It took no longer than a bong or two before the storm cloud of magic was drawn within the Great Working. The tower glowed as bright as it ever had in the Hour, bathing Emily's still body, and the writhing Pooka clan, in a sickly green light. The Nocturne adjusted the shrunken cloak on her shoulders, which could've been mistaken for a normal cape now, if it wasn't for the long black thread of magic that connected it to the tower. She pulled it close around her, to keep out the cold of a world without magic, and moved her hands again.

Now, as the bongs rang out, the oh-so-famous sound warped. It bonged too slowly and too deeply and too . . . sideways. It hurt the ear and the mind at the same time.

The Nocturne was changing the tune, *chaining* the tune. Using her command of music to corrupt the Great Working's purpose and bind the magic to her for ever. Her face was beautiful and terrible, all pretence of humanity fallen away, showing only the stark inner light of a god waiting to be born.

Then the emerald light of the tower changed and flickered into a terrible scarlet. The bells speeded up and the Nocturne's knife-sharp intensity twisted into confusion. This was not in her plan. Her fluid hand gestures became choppy and agitated but the lights of the tower were untouched by her commands. She fought to control the tones of the bells without success.

A snarl spread across the Nocturne's face. She thrashed her arms, trying to alter the music, trying to change the magic, yet nothing was happening. The tower flashed scarlet like an emergency beacon. The stretch of cloak linking the Nocturne and the Great Working sagged, rippled and tossed in the air, utterly out of control. The Nocturne was suddenly dragged forward and stumbled, her icy, proud face now a mask of shock.

The final midnight bong rang out and the scarlet lightning that crackled up and down the tower went out like a plug had been pulled. In the silent darkness that followed, the Nocturne gabbled to herself.

'I primed the Working with magic. I manipulated the

chimes to make it mine.' She shook her head, unable to comprehend. 'And it was exactly midnight.'

From behind her came a terribly familiar voice.

'Aw, man, did it not work? That sucks,' the voice, or perhaps more accurately the gob, said. 'Have you tried turning it off and on again?'

CHAPTER 24

The Nocturne whirled around to find Emily standing behind her, unharmed apart from a football-sized black hole blown straight through her chest.

'*What have you done?!*' the Nocturne howled. 'Why aren't you dead?'

Emily looked down. The hole looked as if it went straight through her, but the blackness inside it glittered with a sprinkling of stars.

'Because I wear Midnight, you rotten git, and it absorbs magic.' She touched the ragged edges of the bomber jacket that concealed Bron's suit and winced. 'That was my favourite, though.'

'You've ruined everything,' the Nocturne snarled. 'If the magic isn't bound at midnight, it will dissipate.' She gave Emily a mad-eyed look. 'You haven't saved anybody. Your people will still die.'

'Who said it was midnight?' said Emily, and couldn't help letting a little grin creep out.

The Nocturne's eyes narrowed with suspicion. She looked up. The sky above, the real sky, was visible now. Her sapphire gaze gauged the position of the stars and moon.

'But it's . . . it's not midnight? How . . . ?'

Emily was definitely grinning now.

'Tell me!' screamed the Nocturne, and glass broke all around the square. 'Tell me how you have changed time!'

'I mean, wow. Talk about a god complex.' Emily shook her head. 'I haven't changed actual time, you cosmic wonk. We just moved the hands forward on the clock.'

'But, but . . .' The Nocturne's face was riven with doubt. A very unfamiliar expression for her. 'You lie. The wrong time couldn't have caused all this.'

'Sure,' said Emily, 'but what if a magical clockwork expert had placed the most cursed coins ever on to the pendulum just as you tried to cast the biggest spell in the world, say?'

The Nocturne gaped in horror at her. 'Sorry about that.' Emily held her hands up, palms out, as if to placate the Older Power. 'Thanks for filling the clock up with all the magic though. Wasn't sure how we were going to manage that bit.'

The Nocturne, her face blank with shock, stared up at the now darkened clock tower.

'You . . . YOU!' She writhed in sheer rage.

'Well, I'd love to stay and chat, but I really have to go now,' said Emily, backing away.

She kept her hands up, higher now, as if the Nocturne was holding a gun on her.

'You think you can surrender? Now? There will be no quarter.'

The light from the Nocturne's eyes cast her face into the shadows of a skull, and the cloak she still wore sparkled with a blaze of stars.

'I said, "I REALLY HAVE TO GO NOW!"' Emily shouted.

As she yelled, the Nocturne twisted and swelled and groaned out into the primal goddess shape she had worn millennia ago. She grew and grew to the deep heartbeat of animal-hide drums. She was all bulk and curves, skin a woad-stained blue, and glowed like metal in a forge. The Nocturne screamed her rage and raised huge blue fists over her head, but before they could crash down there was a flash of black and silver and Emily was gone.

Emily's arms threatened to pop out of their sockets for a second as her dad pulled her aboard the speeding Night

Post bike, then she was sat on the crossbar, safe in his arms. The nightshade clipped to the handlebars fluttered madly as the bike howled vertically up through the dark. Everything blurred around them; they even outran the Nocturne's stone-shattering scream of rage.

'Hello, Puzzle,' said her dad in his calm, quiet voice. 'Try not to wriggle too much. This is quite tricky.' He leant ever so slightly sideways, and the bike arced with him. 'Although it was worse with the werewolf earlier, I must admit.'

A few more terrifying high-speed seconds, and her dad pulled up sedately to the kerb. The kerb in this case was the really-not-that-wide ledge under the enormous white clock face of Big Ben. The gold-and-black chequerboard of the supporting pillars gleamed in the light. She wobbled on the crossbar as the bike hovered.

'You did really well, love. Just hold on until it's done.' He glanced down. 'We'll hold her off now.'

She followed his gaze. Below them, at the base of the clock tower, a vast blue form leapt in the air to grasp onto the outside of the tower. The Nocturne began to haul herself up, roaring in fury.

'Oh man, she's so mad. Be careful.'

He gripped her arm as she dismounted and pressed herself back against the glass. He winked, blew her a kiss, then drew and ignited his flaming sword, falling away into the night like a stone.

She watched him plunge down the dizzying drop, sword blazing like a comet as he dive-bombed the Older Power. As he did, other flames lit up the darkness. Hunts-by-Night, Jonesy, Japonica. All mounted on night-shade-powered flying bikes, each holding a glowing weapon. The Night Post to the rescue! They swooped in and charged at the Nocturne, firing bolts of flame. The Nocturne howled her rage and batted at them with a huge hand as they buzzed her.

Emily could barely stand to watch, but couldn't look away. Leaning over a bit too far, she had a sickening feeling as she started to overbalance, but a hand grabbed her wrist. It was Tarkus, reaching through the glass door in the clock face. His grip on her arm was unshakeable but his eyes were firmly closed.

'Well done. Pleased you're not dead. Can we go inside now?'

He hauled her back into the vast room beyond, the mighty bells hanging above. Not a single piece of clock-work moved. The Great Working had been turned off. The silence was eerie, but the very tower itself throbbed with the stolen power it now contained.

'She's coming for us, Tee. Will we be ready to turn it back on?'

'We're almost there.'

From the door behind him, two angry voices echoed up

the stairs. One a clipped English accent, another broad Irish.

'I think I was quite clear which coin I said to remove.'

'I think 'tis clear yer an eejit!'

'Oh god,' said Emily. 'What's Bron doing?'

'Cornelius assures me they'll be ready in time,' said Tarkus. 'They're just taking the bad pennies off and resetting the pendulum. Ah, see?'

On the giant white clock faces that surrounded them, the enormous hands shuddered backwards to return to exactly midnight. Emily looked at her watch as Tarkus popped the silver cover of his night watch. There were seven minutes to true midnight. Just seven minutes until they could restart the Great Working and, if all miraculously went to plan, the Midnight Hour too.

With a sudden vibration the whole room darkened as a sheen of black fog drifted up from the floor. No, it wasn't fog, it was the sparkling cinder soot of raw magic and it was leaking out of the very stonework of the clock tower and filling the room.

'Umm Tee, should it be doing that?'

The magic was fountaining out of every inch of the tower now, passing through the glass clock faces like they weren't there, and spilling into the night.

A howl of werewolf despondency came from down-stairs, before Cornelius sprinted into the bell room with

Bron right behind him. 'Something is pulling the magic from the clock!' he gasped.

Emily ran to the open panel, and peered down.

'Oh, that is really not good.'

The monstrous form of the Nocturne was still being held at bay by flying bikes, but now the remains of the Midnight cloak she wore rippled with renewed life. Great wings of shadow plumed from her back, and the glittering smoke from the tower was flooding down to her. She was pulling all the magic back in.

'I . . . I totally hadn't planned for that.' Emily bit her lip hard. 'Cornelius, will we still have enough magic to restart the Hour at midnight?'

'We barely had enough before this.' He shook his head. 'If she continues, we'll be undone.'

'Yer a Pooka – steal it back!' yelled Bron, pushing past Cornelius.

'She'll never fall for it again!' said Emily.

Bron poked Emily in the chest, right where the Midnight suit was revealed. 'No, with this. It's just like her cloak. Steal it back!'

Moments later, after handing her joggers and precious hog hoodie to Tarkus, Emily was standing at a precarious angle on the ledge with the Midnight suit fully revealed and flapping in the wind. Below her, the Nocturne was wreathed in a boiling sea of magic, and had driven the attacking bikes away. She climbed towards Emily, hoovering in more magic as she did.

'Oh man, this isn't how it was supposed to go,' muttered Emily but she couldn't think about that now. On Bron's instructions, she somehow had to ignore the approaching doom and concentrate hard on Midnight thoughts. Thoughts about moonlight-silvered pavements and stark shadows. About the Hour, and how she loved it and longed for it, and how much she wanted to keep it and all her people safe.

Without her even noticing, the magic particles started to roll on in. Soon she too was the centre of her own whirlwind of magic. Her suit grew deeper and darker, until she was wearing a black hole that roiled with a cosmic whirl. A terrible howling came from below. She looked down and saw the Nocturne, huge, enraged and closer all the time. Their eyes met.

'This. Is. Mine!' the Nocturne raged. She pointed at Emily with a huge blue hand, then made a grasping motion, as if pulling on an invisible rope. The sooty whirlwind around Emily wavered in mid-air then began to flood downwards instead. Emily felt a lurch and a pull too and, before she could scream, she'd been snatched off the ledge.

She braced herself for a nasty squashy death, but then found she was standing on the face of the tower, looking down, as if gravity was a law that only applied to other people. She remembered Bron running down this very tower, wearing this very . . .

'Suit! Good suit,' she said, patting its shoulder. 'That's two I owe you— Argh!' Another yank from below and she was pulled a few more lurching steps down the tower towards the blue-skinned monstrosity.

Emily dug her heels in and thought as hard as she could to pull the magic towards her. With no magic left in the clock, they fought over what remained as it swirled between them like ink in a whirlpool. She was losing, though. The Nocturne's will was simply stronger. More and more of the magic, vast black clots of it, was streaming away from her as the Nocturne clawed back her stolen treasure. Then real treasure fell, a shower of gold and silver over Emily's shoulder. Accompanied by a screech of pure Irish rage.

'Take that, ya wagon!'

It was Bron, leaning over the ledge and dropping the bad pennies off their chain straight on to the Nocturne. They'd almost destroyed her once, but now she was vastly more powerful. Even so, they made her scream as they landed on her, melting on her skin into puffs of purple smoke and an awful smell of burning metal. As the last coins hit her straight in the face, the Nocturne lost her grip and plunged, howling halfway down the tower before her claws brought her to a screeching halt.

'I couldn't think of what else to do,' Bron said.

'That was perfect,' said Emily, beaming up at her. Then came a teeny-tiny sound that chilled her blood. It was the alarm going off on her digital watch. It was almost midnight, the real one this time.

Nerves on fire with electric panic, she ran straight back up the sheer wall. Bron dived out of the way as Emily threw herself inside.

'Cornelius, TURN IT ON!'

Even as she spoke, the clockwork arms started to whir, and the quarter bells chimed out. It was too loud to hear, but she could see Tarkus was reciting the words of the Night Folk's quarter-chime prayer.

'All through this night, moon be my faith, and by its light, all shall be safe.'

The chimes finished and a luminous green witchlight started to flicker outside the great glass walls. The Great Working had awoken, but it needed magic if it was going to work.

'Do we have enough?' said Tarkus.

'I just don't know! The Nocturne took so much,' said Emily, 'I don't even know how to put it back in!' and then it was too late because the great main bell was ringing. Big Ben tolling twelve, the one and only time that they would have a chance to restart the spell and save the Midnight Hour.

BONG!

Somehow, she had to get the magic out of the suit and into the Great Working. Emily closed her eyes and groped with her mind for something she could use, the same way she reached for her luck or other forms. She reached within for the suit's inner pocket of magic. There was something there, throbbing with life.

BONG!

Without hesitating she gritted her teeth and grabbed hold. It was like gripping on to a live electricity cable. Such incredible power. Jolts of energy coursed through her and, eyes still closed, she could see the true Great Working now. It was a shining construction of gold and emerald green. Within it, an absence waiting to be filled. With everything she had left, she poured the magic from the suit into it. It was like pushing her luck but on a cosmic scale.

BONG!

Even as she did it, she knew. The hole was too deep, and she had nowhere near enough magic.

She opened her eyes and the clock tower shook and vibrated. The emerald light of the Great Working's enchantment lit up brighter for a second or two then fizzled and went out. Tarkus was staring at her and all she could do was shake her head helplessly. All of this and they were still going to lose.

BONG!

Big Ben rang out with an awful discordancy. That terrible sound she'd heard earlier while playing dead. The Nocturne corrupting the spell again, making it her own.

BONG!

Emily heard a voice then. It couldn't have been her mum, she was too far away, yet even so, she heard, clear as day, her mum say, 'Emily, remember the rule!'

Never leave home without your hedgehog.

BONG!

As the bells rang out to mark the end of the world, she ran to her ruined hoodie and gently removed her warm, spiky, small-footed friend.

'Hog, I really, really need your help.'

He blinked one eye open, and gave her a beady look along his pointed black nose.

BONG!

She walked towards the open panel in the clock face, towards fresh air and the night. She spoke close to his ear because of the bells.

'Look, I'm not daft. You're weirdly heavy in between dimensions and the Antler Lady called you "kinsman".'

Hoggins didn't say anything, but he was a hedgehog after all.

BONG!

Below her, over her, through her, the Nocturne shrieked triumph.

'Hog, if you're who I think you are, then you can't help unless an ancient law has been broken, can you?'

She thought he frowned at that, but it was hard to say what a hedgehog's expressions truly meant.

BONG!

'So, I'm telling you that an ancient law has been broken – she is taking more than she needs.'

He hadn't even twitched. She thought her heart might stop.

'She's taking everything, and all the Night Folk, all the Pooka, my family who have helped you, will die.'

BONG!

'Hoggins, if the world ends, then that means no more biscuits. Apocalypse equals zero snacks. Which should also be a crime, right?'

His spines definitely prickled. He might have sighed.

BONG!

She looked over the ledge and the Nocturne was right below her now, suspended in a storm of seething black light as she wrestled to bind the magic to her and her alone, for ever.

Emily had a horrible flashback to when she had tried to get help from the Hog before, and ended up being just a girl holding a hedgehog.

'Oh god, I hope I'm right. You better not just be "probably magical", sunshine, I'm telling you.'

BONG!

Emily held the Hog up and out. As the great old bell Big Ben gave tongue to the twelfth and final chime, midnight was struck, the Nocturne screamed in victory and . . .

. . . a hedgehog sneezed.

CHAPTER 25

Emily felt the sneeze on her palm. A distinct *achoo* . . . and everything changed.

There was an overwhelming smell of autumn leaves. The Hog, while cupped in her palms, was also immense and heavy and everywhere. Vast and unknowable, yet a rustle unseen in the undergrowth. He was in the woods but also *was* the woods. He was the heart of the world and her pocket friend too. She hovered in that wood between the worlds for eons, or it might have been just a breath, until she heard a sigh. Then, with a blink, the Hog was small, vast, in her hands, in every blade of grass, then gone.

She snapped back to the end of the world, and Tarkus grabbed at her to stop her tumbling from the ledge. Her hands were empty. She looked frantically for the Hog in case she'd dropped him, but he wasn't there. The clock tower started to flicker, like a cranky fluorescent tube coming on. Then it lit up like a beacon as the emerald luminescence of magic coruscated up and down it. The whole tower vibrated like a rocket waiting to launch. Someone had given the world a nudge, just enough magic to restart the greatest spell ever made and set right an injustice. Now, the Great Working was doing what it had been built to do, pulling in every shred of magic into a place outside of time to keep it safe.

A scream high enough to shatter tooth enamel came from below. Emily crawled to the edge and looked down. The Nocturne was still there, still aloft, but was being thrashed and whipped back and forth. Her cloak was no longer great wings, but a thin slice of darkness tied around her neck being pulled inexorably into the clock. She fought it but she was a fisherman who'd caught a whale. She screamed with rage as she was scraped against the glowing walls of the tower. Emily felt the unbearable static pressure of a storm about to break. She shouted down to the Nocturne.

'You've got to let it go. You've got to!'

The Nocturne's great sapphire eyes had the clarity of madness.

'I will never let go. I will never give in.'

They were the last words Emily ever heard her say. An enormous bolt of green lightning shot up from the clock tower. It arced up to fill the entire sky with a glow that would put the Northern Lights to shame. The lightning leapt from the tower across the tautly drawn cable of the cloak of Midnight magic and into the Older Power wearing it. Without even time to scream, the Nocturne simply burst into a blaze of white light and disintegrated.

There was a period of blackness then, during which there was a sound like someone slurping the very last of a giant milkshake through an infinitely long straw. Enormous unseen forces pulled at Emily, spinning her up into the cosmos, the universe flapping around her like a ragged thread, and it was all so much that she thought she was going to pop until . . .

. . . it stopped.

Emily opened her eyes to find herself sprawled out on the floor. She wasn't sure when that had happened. She could see the Great Working towering in front of her, so she wasn't up there anymore either. She was back in Parliament Square again.

In the next moment she felt the ripple of magic pass through her. The clouds above streamed away like a video on rewind, and the great full moon hove back into view, filling the square with its bright cold light. As the silvered beams touched her face, she knew it had worked.

They were back in the Midnight Hour. They were home.

Emily shut her eyes again and decided she'd stay on the floor. It was reassuringly flat, even if she was oddly chilly.

'You should probably get up or you'll get swept away with the other rubbish,' said Tarkus from above her.

'Excellent "you are also rubbish" implication there, Flowers. Ten points to Hufflepuff.' She blinked open her eyes. 'You didn't understand it, but I just double-dissed you there.'

'I have no doubt.' He sank down beside her, his colour back to its normal healthy olive-wood sheen. He quirked an eyebrow at her. 'I'm loath to ask, but you're aware you no longer have trousers, yes?'

Oh god, not again.

She looked down. The Midnight suit had gone, vanished as if it never were. She sat up, tugging at the long T-shirt she'd thankfully been wearing beneath it.

'Jaysus, love, put 'em away,' came her mum's voice. Emily turned, and some velvety cloth hit her in the face.

'Put these on, afore ye frighten the wee man.'

Her mum had thrown her some actually rather snazzy black velvet trousers with a shiny stripe down the side.

They'd coordinate nicely with her flaming-red face. She was already struggling into them before realization dawned.

'Hang on, why have you got spare trous— Oh no!'

She looked up at Maeve, who was wearing a particularly good silk top hat and a very flouncy black coat.

'Mum! These are Dead people's clothes!'

'Ahh, it's not like they're using them, now, is it?'

Maeve had the baby in her arms and was looking very pleased with her haul from the vampiric boot sale.

'Are you okay? Is Mammy? Where's Dad?!'

'Ahh, we're all good. Hang on.' Maeve ferreted around under her brightly coloured hair and extracted a big pink foam plug from her ear. 'Wouldn't have been too clever if'n we didn't all have these though. Good shout.'

She was trying to juggle the baby so she could reach her other ear. Emily held her hands out.

'Here, I'll have Jesse.'

Her mum raised an eyebrow but handed him over. His little fur-covered face and long black-tipped ears popped out of the blanket as she took him. She held him gently to her and, with a sigh and a wriggle, he changed back to human form and eyed her curiously with his big blue eyes.

'All right?' she said to her brother. He didn't reply but snuggled in against her and started to snore. He was, she supposed, quite a nice little chap really. She sniffed the top of his head. Definitely the best end.

'Well, that's the world saved then,' said her dad, limping over. He had an arm in a sling and looked very bruised, but his beaming smile was untouched. 'Good job all round.'

He clapped Emily on the shoulder. 'You're totally grounded, by the way.'

'What for?!' squawked Emily.

'Going on an adventure without asking permission.'

'But that was ages ago, and . . . I was kidnapped by a magic owl!'

'Oh, the old magic owl excuse, eh?' said her mum. 'Cuts no ice round here.'

Emily pointed an accusatory finger at her mum. 'I think what we actually need to discuss is the lifetime of lying you've been doing about the Hog.'

'I told you, I can't . . .' Her mum paused, and then opened and closed her mouth a few times and smacked her tongue as if she'd tasted something funny. 'Oh, grand, the secrets spell has broken. Must have happened when he showed ye hisself. I can tell ye now.' She readjusted her top hat as she spoke. 'I met him on an adventure long ago, did him a favour or three an' he's been keeping an eye on the family ever since.'

'And he was an actual Ancient Power! A nature god!' Emily's voice was getting louder. 'Which not only did you fail to mention, but in fact specifically said he was just a hedgepig!'

'Well, mostly, he *was* just a hedgepig.' Maeve waved a dismissive hand.

'He just changed the whole world!' Emily shouted.

'He wasn't much of a god these days though. He'd had enough, you see. Just wanted to be a hedgehog. Can ye blame him?' Her mum sighed and slipped an arm around her dad. 'And ye is what ye are – the longer ye're a hedgehog, the more hoggy ye become.' She gave Emily a wink. 'He must have really liked ye to do what he did.'

Emily felt a stab of sadness.

'He's gone now, hasn't he?'

Her mum pulled her over for a comforting squeeze.

'Aye, maybe. He always hated a fuss.'

Behind them, there was a gasp from Tarkus. Clip-clopping across the square towards them was Painty. Holding her bridle and leaning heavily on her was a tall, thin figure with long umber hair, from under which shone eyes of a thousand shifting colours that glowed in the night.

'Art!' yelled Emily. 'But, but . . .'

'Knew it, I did!' said Maeve. 'Ye sent the horse, didn't ye?'

'Oh!' gasped Emily. 'It was you who warned me about the hunting hands with the Abbits, wasn't it?'

Art inclined her head to Emily, then drew close to Maeve and took her hand. They looked at each other but did not speak, an unreadable smile on Art's face.

'Ye were hurt again, weren't ye?' Tears ran down her mum's cheeks as she held her best beloved's hand. 'Thanks for trying tae look after her, anyway.'

After a long while in which Emily had a pronounced urge to busy herself with talking nonsense to Jesse, Art and Maeve let each other go.

Tarkus drew himself up and gave a particularly princely and formal bow.

'Ma'am, I understand that you will desire your fine steed back.' He reached into a pocket and proffered a handful of small squares of paper. 'May I please leave you with these sugar cube drawings that I have . . .'

He trailed off in shock as Art gently took his hand in both of hers and folded his fingers back over the offered drawings. She patted his hand before releasing him.

'Erm, I . . .'

Art smiled and walked away, leaving Painty standing there.

'She means you can keep Painty, doofus,' said Emily. She didn't think she'd ever seen him smile so much.

Emily followed Art, still juggling her snoozy brother. The Older Power was looking up at the Great Working, her face as enigmatic as ever. Emily gave herself a swift internal lecture about not saying anything about 'blown up' or 'exploded', then joined her.

'I'm so sorry you're the only one left. If you want to come and stay with us, you can.' She had the nasty feeling her mouth was moving without her brain being involved. 'We've got lots of sculptures and stuff.'

She was already aware this was possibly a bad idea. Where would they keep the immortal personification of art? In the shed?

Art looked up and gave Emily a small half-smile, the delicate silver tracery of scars on her face moving into a new arrangement as she did, like snow crystals across her cheek. She dipped her head once, quickly, then shook it. *Thank you, but no.* Then she pointed with one long slender finger.

A whirlwind was approaching them. It was a black spinning cone shot through with green flashes. As it drew near to them, staggering Emily with its backdraught, she could see that it was made up of the black ink of millions of tiny words, interlaced with an endless series of zeros and ones all in electric green glowing type.

The whirlwind coalesced into a woman.

She was extremely tall, and wore a crisp white shirt, black trousers and vivid red lipstick. Her long black hair plumed back to reveal a sleek undercut, and her eyes sparked with green light. Her rolled-up shirt sleeves revealed olive skin covered in the black ink of tattooed words that seemed to move and change even as Emily watched.

It was the Library.

'But! But! I thought you were—' Emily burst into tears and ran to hug her.

The Library raised a very surprised eyebrow as her waist was grabbed by a sniffling Pooka and a gurgling baby. She gave Emily one firm squeeze, then stepped back.

'Fret not. I am well. Perhaps, even . . . all good?' She smacked her lips as if tasting the flavour of the unusual words.

Emily scrubbed at her blub-face as she eyed the Library, who was now arm in arm with Art.

'You're okay, but you're . . . all different.'

'Death is an awfully big adventure. We are not always the same when we return.'

The Library held an arm out as if to appraise herself and gave a very satisfied nod. The tattooed words on her skin crawled into new sentences to please her as she did.

'In the brief time we spent in your world, I found a new source of words to feed on.' Her usually ink-black eyes sparked green again. 'I believe you call it the internet.'

'Whoa,' said Emily.

'I now appear to be much more fond of cats than before.'

'Well, big thumbs-up on the makeover,' said Emily. 'But I'm going to miss the quoting.'

'Don't judge a book by its cover, hmmm?' said the Library, and actually winked at Emily.

'If you don't really die, does that mean that the Nocturne might come back?'

The Library frowned. 'Perhaps. She put herself upon the anvil of great forces, though, and has fallen between worlds.'

Art gestured at her sister, her fingers painting the air with colour.

'Yes, exactly,' said the Library. 'We will try and find her, for no matter what she has done, she is still our family.'

The sisters stood together, an LED-green spark gaze and another of a whole painter's palette of colours both looking at Emily. She tried not to fidget.

'We thank you, Emily Featherhaugh Connolly. You and all of your clan, and allies. You have done a great thing here. We shall never forget.'

Together, they inclined their heads in a bow of thanks. Emily shuffled a bit, but an undeniable swell of something that might have been pride filled her with warmth.

'We have been borne back ceaselessly into the past, but now we must move forward into the broad moonlit uplands of the future.'

As the Library spoke, her words briefly appeared on her arms then vanished again.

'This sanctuary will now need new leadership and wise guidance,' said the Library. Emily opened her mouth to say something but – 'Neither of which you are remotely qualified to provide,' the Library continued.

Emily closed her mouth and nodded. *Fair enough*.

'Worthy Folk will be appointed, but even so, know that our watch over this Midnight Hour will never again falter, we promise,' the Library said as Art smiled and nodded. 'But now, things to do, kitties to stroke. LOL.'

The Library and Art raised their joined hands together over their heads, and in a blink of colour, they were gone, leaving only a shower of red hearts and yellow smiling faces that fizzed then vanished.

'Wow, Jesse,' said Emily, shaking her head. 'She is actually even stranger this way.'

Tarkus joined her, his arm draped over Painty's neck as he fed her sugar cube drawings. They looked over the square. Where a riot had once happened, now an impromptu party had broken out. Pat had magicked up a fiddle from somewhere, and now Night Folk jumped, flapped, howled and hooted in a mad joy at the sight of the restored moon. Emily's mum and dad appeared to be dancing a tango, that had probably been banned in Latin America for being too suggestive, while a normally dignified Pooka clan matriarch swung a big fur coat over her head as she danced a jig with a ghûl princess (thrice removed).

'What now, Flowers? The world's not ending for once.'

'Indeed. I don't quite know what to do with myself

without an overwhelming sense of dread.' He rubbed Painty's nose. 'Someone needs to look after the city and the people though, and that is after all what a polis does.' He nodded over her shoulder. 'The world may not be ending, but things look very different out there.'

They looked around. The Midnight Hour was restored. The moon shone and the clock tower crackled with the comforting emerald light of sorcery within its fog, yet things were not the same. The gas lamps were still there but modern-looking street lamps were mixed in with them, to the delight of the fairies. The skyline had changed too. The great majority of it was still Victorian London, but here and there, a skyscraper loomed. One of them already had a proactive dragon couple building a nest on top. The spell had restored the London of 1859, but it had captured a chunk of the modern-day city too.

'Blimey,' said Emily. 'That's going to be . . . different. Maybe I can come and help out?'

Tarkus looked like he was about to say something withering, then paused. 'Maybe you can. We clearly need a consulting expert on modernity.'

'Sold,' said Emily. 'I think you should come and look at some more trees in the daylight too. If you've got time and all that.'

'I'd like that. After all, now we have all the time in the world.' A sweet herbal scent filled the air.

They smiled companionably at each other and would, perhaps, have spoken more, but a shopping trolley piled up with imps roared in between them, towed by a purple boar tethered to the front, pursued by a howling pack of gnolls mounted on mini-scooters.

The future, apparently, was going to be interesting.

As Emily entered her bedroom after the longest day in history, she'd never felt so exhausted. The sight of her comfy bed, favourite blanket and, of course, the green magnificence of the Feesh was like paradise. She dropped everything where she was standing, hurling socks and fancy velvet pantaloons over chairs and piles of books without even looking. She walked to the bed in her best zombie lurch and was about to fall face first into it when she heard a tiny noise behind her. A scritch and a faint buzzing vibration. She froze, cranking her already half-closed eyes back open.

The noise was coming from the pile of cardboard boxes and tubes that formed the hog-palace. She crept over and placed her ear against the side of the big sleeping area, formed from an old shoe box. The vibration came again. Her heart stopped beating and her stomach clenched as she ever so gently peered within.

Inside, curled up amongst the warmth of the shavings

and hay, was a very familiar small, round and brown form, all covered in prickles, and snoring like a much larger animal.

Hoggins was home.

'Adventure buddy,' she whispered happily. She rummaged in her satchel and dropped in an emergency biscuit, just in case he woke up hungry, then took herself off to bed. She had plans to hibernate herself.

CODA

And somewhere, in a time outside of time, in a blank and formless void, a musical note of purest tone sounded, and a pair of sapphire-blue eyes opened, and looked upon the absence of world they found themselves in.

There had been something, something very important to them, but ... they could not remember it now. Perhaps it was for the best. It was, they thought, time for a new tune.

They looked upon the endlessness of the new realm and around them music came into being in the air, light trilling sounds that spoke of peace and joy.

Amidst the music, they could sense something else now: a feeling of people, no, *family*, who cared for them, searching for them. They were far, far away, but even in the void, their love was like a beacon.

The Symphony smiled gently, then set off on the long journey back towards the light, whistling as she went.

ACKNOWLEDGEMENTS

'But all you did was list our families and friends,' said Tarkus.
'I know,' she said. 'Who else do we ever need?'

From Trindles:

I'm so thankful to the pockets of people in my life who cheer me on. If I needed to save the world, I reckon I could assemble the winning team. With Trinders, Wildgeese, Zarkoffs, Swaggers, Tribe Girls, Waterstoners and Bobians by my side, no big bad would stand a chance.

The biggest thanks of all goes to Ben, my very own adventure buddy. We wrote a trilogy! How magical. It seems like just yesterday we were called to adventure and now we're tucked back in our Hobbit holes. Safe, fed, and only slightly traumatized by the whole thing. Let's do it again!

From Read:

Books are not written in isolation. Even if the hours at the desk are spent alone, there is always a supporting web of hands and hearts just out of sight. I'd be nothing without mine, both family and friends (you totally know who you are, don't make me do an Oscars speech), and I'm sorry I've been saying 'I'd love to, but I've got a deadline,' for well over a decade now.

Also, I am truly not an isolated writer, because I get to work with Laura, to whom no thanks would ever be enough. Fellow traveller, boon companion, and opposite seat on the see-saw of doom and delight that is writing for a living. I don't know what I'd do without you. We should probably write another book together immediately so I don't have to find out.

From Trindles & Read:

An enormous thank you to all the good eggs at Chicken House.

To Rachel Leyshon, our Story Mage, we thank you for your endless kind-hearted support. There's no one else we'd rather discuss the intricacies of a front wedgie with.

To Elinor, seeing Emily and Hoggins travel the world is the most marvellous thing and we have you to thank. We're so grateful.

To the magic art team who make our books so beautiful. Rachel Hickman, Hannah Peck, and Steve Wells. Thank you for successfully sending our stories out into a world that always judges a book by its cover.

To Jazz, Myers, Sarah, and Esther, thank you for putting up with us and being so wonderful.

Most of all to Barry, the *definitely* magical hedgehog in our publishing pocket. Your enthusiasm and support from the very start, when the Hour was nothing more than extemporary waffle and hand-waving, will never be forgotten.

OI! BOOKFACES! An extra big thank you to you: the librarians, the booksellers, the teachers, the bloggers and reviewers. Our stories would be in the dark without you.